THE
GAME
⊀ OF ⊁
SUNKEN
PLACES

THE
GAME
⊰ OF ⊱
SUNKEN
PLACES

M. T. ANDERSON

SCHOLASTIC PRESS
• NEW YORK •

Copyright © 2004 by M. T. Anderson

Library of Congress Cataloging-in-Publication Data
Anderson, M.T.
The Game of Sunken Places /
M. T. Anderson—1st ed.
p.   cm.
Summary: When two boys stay with an eccentric relative at
his mansion in rural Vermont, they discover an old-fashioned board game
that draws them into a mysterious adventure.
ISBN 0-439-41660-4 (hardcover)—
ISBN 0-439-41661-2 (pbk)
[1. Games—Fiction.   2. Vermont—Fiction.]
I. Title.
PZ7.A54395 Gam 2004
[Fic]—dc22
2003020055

10   9   8   7   6   5   4   3   2   1
04   05   06   07   08

Printed in the United States of America   37
First edition, July 2004

text type Excelsior

Typography by Steve Scott

*To all those authors
who showed me that evil
could be fought while on vacation,
wearing knee-socks.*

PROLOGUE

The woods were silent, other than the screaming. It was a summer's night. Nothing in the forest moved. Somewhere in the darkness, things wailed hoarsely.

There were miles of empty pathway rambling past old logging trails and older ruins. There were aisles of trees, motionless. The blind river ran through the shadows. And crouched, listening in the bracken, his breath fast and frightened, was a real estate developer. He wore shorts, and a T-shirt that read, ME, A CHOWDERHEAD?

He should not have come into the woods. There were signs marked NO TRESPASSING by the road. The signs were so old that the trees had grown around them, and gray vines laced their edges like witch macrame. Signs like that, these woods devoured.

But Milton Deatley had paid no attention to the signs. He liked to walk in the forest by night and picture it his. He liked to dream of bulldozing the trees, leaving wide tracks where the messy scrub now grew. He pictured the forest cut down and subdivided into smooth lanes full of luxury homes with carpeted rec rooms, with Peg-Board tool racks in the garages, with walk-in freezers and sauna baths, with concrete elk out on the lawn. He wanted this land to develop. In his brain, he called his estates *Rumbling Elk Haven*.

He had been walking for an hour through the stillness when he heard the screaming. The woods were silent, and there could be no mistake. This was not something misheard.

It was something evil.

In the moment that he first heard it, it seemed to him that nothing else existed: nothing but darkness, and heat drizzling off the leaves, and the sound of several human voices howling.

Carefully, he moved through the woods. He knew the paths well, because he had strolled there in the day. He had named them things in his mind, things they would be called when they were paved. He liked it when paved spaces — roads, cul-de-sacs, rotaries — were named after baseball stars, or vice presidents, or girls who refused to go out with him in middle school.

The path was coated with needles. His tread was soft on them. The screaming did not stop. Sometimes it was only one voice. At those times, it sounded like a man screaming in falsetto. Sometimes it sounded like several people, all being cut with different instruments.

The boughs of the trees were perfectly still. None of

VIII

them moved. A bird was motionless on a branch, its eye open. The moon was not bright.

Milton Deatley saw a light through the forest.

Carefully, he moved toward it. He put down his feet quietly, but there were twigs on the path that snapped.

The light was a fire. He could see the rippling shadows of flame.

He walked toward it, crouched.

He came to the verge of a clearing in the pines. He huddled there, squatting close to the ground, ready to run.

The fire was from an abandoned snowmobile. Someone had poured oil on it and had thrown on a match. It lit up the clearing. By its light, Milton Deatley could see the screaming ritual.

There was a mound, a tall, steep hillock, and on its sides were scattered people in robes, with hoods that hid their faces. Their arms were stiff at their sides. Their mouths could be seen when they opened them to scream.

Before them stood a figure in a robe. He had some kind of tablet, a mystical tablet, lying before him, and he pointed to it by the light of the burning Ski-doo. Each time he pointed to a different square on the tablet, someone new shrieked. It seemed like an alien kind of singing. Then the keening-master would raise his hand, and pour more oil on the fire from a watering can. The fire would flare.

Milton squinted at the tablet. Now he saw that it was actually a game. A board game, with spaces to move pieces, and spots to put stacks of cards. It was open on an old Formica-topped kitchen table. The table's legs were rusted.

The conductor touched spaces on the board. The eerie choir cried.

Milton watched them. Their voices intertwined. Some shrieked one note; some gasped; others wailed strange sighs.

From behind the mound, from out of the shadows, several more figures came. They carried the limp figure of a woman.

Her head rolled back. Her hair hung down limply.

"She is finished," said one of the men who carried her.

"Indeed," said the conductor with the game.

Milton Deatley's heart beat in panic.

The group with the woman moved toward the fire.

And Milton turned to run.

He pushed aside branches and jumped toward the path. He heard a scuffling behind him. He was on the path now, barreling as quickly as he could go toward the road. His chest felt giddy and queasy. Twigs slapped at his face.

A small man was standing on a stump, saying to him, "Now things will not go well for you."

He found himself in a maze of mounds. He scrambled from gully to gully. He clawed at the needles and loam and catapulted over rises. He slid down knolls. He could not hear if anyone pursued him.

He broke out into open woodland. There were lights floating through the trees. Perhaps insects. Deatley kicked up leaves as he ran.

He kept thinking: *This is no joke.*

✕

Deatley paused in the midst of the wood. He was on a slope. He realized he was running up the mountain, not down toward the road. The bonfire lay between him and his SUV. He was trapped.

As he stood there and pondered this, he heard hunting horns.

Someone was coming down the mountain. Someone with many legs.

Horses.

Riders.

Weapons. Things made of metal.

They were all around him.

He fell on his knees.

And still, from the forest, they came in droves.

PART ONE

⊙NE

The envelope was outlined in gold leaf and addressed in Gothic script. Nothing else that came in the mail that day was of particular interest. Bills with plastic windows. Three unwanted record club selections. Catalogs selling button-down oxford shirts for men, in colors like yucca, furze, and jungle burgundy. There was considerable curiosity about the Gothic letter by the time Gregory Buchanan ripped it open.

Later that day, he showed it to his friend Brian. They were having burgers.

"Look what I got."

"What is it?" asked Brian.

"Invitation," said Gregory. His mouth was full. "From my uncle Max up in Vermont."

"Why all the gold lettering?"

"He's strange, Uncle Max." Gregory shook his head. "Probably insane. He lives in kind of a different world from the rest of us. You know? The kind of world where electricity is a lot of invisible spiders. The kind of world where there's organ music that gets louder when he eats refined sugar."

Brian smiled and nodded.

"So," said Gregory, "I'm supposed to go up to his place in Vermont for a while. To visit him and my cousin Prudence." Gregory squelched some ketchup onto his plate. "The letter says I have to bring 'a companion.'" Gregory opened up the note. "Well, it says, 'a companion for your amusement, so long as he be of solid reputation and respectful and unspotted demeanor.'" Gregory handed the note to Brian. He explained, "You're the only one of my friends who's house-trained."

Brian, pudgy and dark-haired, looked at the letter through his glasses. He read, half-muttering, "'. . . to enjoy the salutary effects of the bucolic landscape and air untrammeled by the effluents and insalubrities of the urban crush.'"

"You're the smart one," said Gregory. "Can you translate?"

"I think it means that the countryside is healthy and the city is dirty. Does he always talk like this?"

"I don't know. I only met him once."

"I'd," said Brian, shrugging, "I'd like to go."

"I'm inviting you. You don't need to be timid."

"I'd like to."

"I'm warning you, he's strange."

"It will . . . I guess . . . it will be an adventure."

"Oh, sure. It'll be weird. Very weird."

Brian smiled. "I don't want to miss it."

4

"No. So that's that."

"Okay," said Brian. "Okay. Now I'm going to order another Fanta."

They couldn't know what an adventure it would be. Already, things were waiting in the hills. Things were hiding in the bushes by the dingy lights of rural Halt'N'Buys, traveling on their strange and lonely pilgrimages.

Things had issued invitations.

✳   ✳   ✳

Gregory Buchanan and Brian Thatz had been best friends for many of their thirteen years. No one could figure out why, or how. The differences between the two were obvious at first glance: Gregory was slim and fair-haired, with a smirk that suggested his flippancy and wit; Brian was stockier, with wire-framed glasses and dark hair, and a quiet frown that suggested he was the more thoughtful and pensive of the two. Gregory was popular, even though (or perhaps because) almost nothing he said made sense. Brian made a lot of sense, but hardly anyone but Gregory ever heard what he had to say. Others didn't see how they got along. Gregory said it was like they were two lobes of the same brain.

When they were in groups, at school or out with the rest of their friends, Gregory kept up a steady flow of talk. Brian hung back shyly, but he often saw things no one else saw. They were inseparable. It was assumed they would spend their school's October vacation together.

Very soon, they had made arrangements with their

parents to travel by train up to Gerenford, Vermont, where they would be picked up by Uncle Max for two weeks' stay in the Green Mountains. Mrs. Thatz, Brian's mother, could only comment that, "At this time of year, the view will be lovely! You'll be there for the changing leaves!" She then lapsed into an autumnal rapture about oranges and reds and fading yellows while Mr. Thatz passed out more mashed potatoes.

So three weeks after the letter arrived, the two were standing in North Station in Boston, waiting for the 8:47 train. The sun was particularly bright that day as the two squinted down the tracks, standing by their overstuffed suitcases. Brian examined the various stickers on Gregory's suitcase. He asked, "Hey — you've never been to Algiers. Have you? Or Sri Lanka? Or Salzburg?"

"No," said Gregory. "Actually, this is my cousin Prudence's. You'll meet her up at Uncle Max's. She lives there and takes care of things for him."

"Whose side of your family are they on?"

"Uncle Max isn't on either side," Gregory explained. "He's not related. Prudence's parents — my aunt and uncle — died when she was seventeen or so. Uncle Max was a good friend of my real uncle. After her parents died, Prudence went to live with him. Before that, though, she traveled all over the world."

"Is she nice?"

"I guess so. I like her, but she's very boring. She doesn't really make jokes. That's one thing you'll notice about her. Really nice, and has the sense of humor of a brick. But, you'll meet her."

Brian nodded, scuffled his sneaker on the concrete, then peered down the track.

The 8:47 arrived at 9:23. With a hiss and a screech, the train slowed to a halt and shot its doors open. The acrid smell of burning rubber and oily steel drifted through the air. There was quite a large crowd waiting to get on. Seating was tight in the train cars. Finally, they found two seats facing each other and heaved their luggage up on the rack above them. With a jerk, the train rolled off to the west.

For about an hour, Brian occupied himself with a 1930s detective novel in which people fired off rounds in alleyways and spoke out of the sides of their mouths, saying things like, "I'm falling for that dame real hard, like a bicyclist in a big, spiked pit." Gregory played handheld Foosball.

The train rumbled on through Massachusetts and Vermont, passing far western towns whose names were, to Bostonians, merely legends. The vistas grew more and more expansive, the landscapes continually more rolling and uneven, until finally the Green Mountains rose into sight. The train wound through vast wooded valleys, past cliffs that had been blasted from the stone to make chasms for the dwarfed highways. Through the window they could see nothing but unending forests and pine-covered hills, mellow in the glow of early fall.

When Brian next looked up, the train was almost empty. People had stepped off at earlier, more suburban stops. There were only a few people left.

One of them was staring straight at him.

Brian looked up meekly and tried to see the man's face. The man was hiding slightly behind an old lady's plastic rain-hood. He was dressed in an old tweed over-coat, a black leather cap pulled down over his forehead. His face was thin, his eyes sunken.

Brian nervously dropped his gaze back to *A Dirk on Thirty-Third Street,* where Archie Temple was hanging off the side of a hotel, pummeling a thug with one hand and reading his prayer beads with the other.

Out of the corner of his eye, Brian saw the man draw something out of his pocket.

Something that glittered with blades.

TWO⊙

The man held a bladed yo-yo. The string was silver. The blades glinted around the yo-yo's edge. Staring at Brian, the man let it drop once, beckoned, and drew it back up into his hand. He had not been harmed. He kept on with his yo-yoing. The metal edges flashed. He did not seem to notice the yo-yo in his hand, he was so intent on peering at Brian.

Brian pretended to read.

The man sat back in his chair. He wound the string of the yo-yo around his fingers. He stared. His fingers were tightly wrapped. He did not seem to notice. His fingers were turning white. Where the yo-yo string was wrapped around them, they had a tinge of red.

After scanning a few pages in a distracted, disjointed manner, Brian looked up again. The man was rising from his seat. The yo-yo string went slack around his fingers. His hands were purple now from the lack of circulation, webbed with white where the string had bitten into the flesh.

Brian squirmed. He kicked the sole of Gregory's sneaker. Gregory was intent on his game. Brian kicked him again.

Gregory said, "Cut it out."

Glaring at Brian, the man shook out one hand, then the other. He closed and opened his fists.

He walked toward Brian. Brian froze in his seat. He was terrified.

The man was beside them. He looked down at Gregory, and then at Brian, and smiled.

Brian didn't know what to do.

The man walked on down the aisle. He staggered past the conductor into the train car.

Gregory was looking out at the hills, his face reflected in the glass. "It makes you want to travel, doesn't it?" he asked. "I mean, I see mountains like this and I want to do something exciting when I'm older."

"Gregory," whispered Brian. "Did you see that guy? With the yo-yo?"

"I'm talking about my life," said Gregory. He raised his hand poetically. "Someday, I want to be a shower curtain repairman."

"This guy was staring at us. He had this bladed yo-yo."

"See, you have your rich fantasy life to get you through the day. But me . . ."

"He was sitting right over there."

"For me, shower curtain repair offers exactly the right mixture of high adventure and mental challenge. Just right for the man who likes his La-Z-Boy with the footrest flipped up."

"I'm not kidding."

Gregory craned his neck around. "Why didn't you tell me when he was there?"

"I didn't want to attract his attention."

"I can understand that."

They stared at the spot where he had sat — but there was no one sitting there now.

The train galloped on, over miles of tracks.

Finally, as the day grew dim, the train skidded into Gerenford, a town whose only conspicuous feature was a huge marble monolith dedicated to the town's founder, a man who'd settled down at the spot when he'd found that his tent pegs were stuck. The two friends lumbered off the train with their bulky luggage and watched the last car snake away to the north.

"There. That man," whispered Brian, grabbing Gregory's arm and tugging him. "Into the snack bar."

"What? He went into the snack bar?"

"No. Walking right there."

"Because, Brian, people are allowed to go to the snack bar."

"He was the one staring at us on the train."

The man was walking toward the station exit. He carried two strangely shaped valises.

"Him?" said Gregory.

"It was weird. It's like he knew us."

Gregory smiled. "Cool."

"Come on!" Brian whispered urgently.

They walked quickly into the little restaurant next to the station. "He was watching us?" said Gregory.

"Yes."

"With a bladed yo-yo?"

"Yes."

"Huh. Funny that kind of thing would catch on."

"I think it was some kind of martial arts device."

"Hate to think what he could do with a Slinky."

Brian frowned. "You're not taking this seriously."

"Calm down," said Gregory. "It'll be fine. Hey, the junk food's on me."

He ordered a Coke and a bag of Funyuns. Brian ordered some fries. They sat for a while on the swiveling stools, waiting for Uncle Max, peering through the windows. The man with the dark-rimmed eyes had walked off down the street, without even turning to look at them.

The elderly man who ran the place picked up a sugar dispenser and wiped the green, speckled counter beneath it. "You watching for someone?"

"Yeah," said Gregory. "My uncle."

"Oh. Ah. He live up here?"

"Well, yeah. I guess he lives on the outskirts of town."

"Mm. What's the name?"

"Maximilian Grendle," said Gregory. "We're going out to his house."

The thin old man slammed down the sugar and looked at the two penetratingly. As he spoke, the crags in his face shifted and darkened. "I'd get . . . you just go now and get on that train and go back to wherever you came from."

Brian glanced up, surprised.

"What?" said Gregory. "What do you mean?"

"If you're smart, you'll leave. No one in Gerenford

12

would go near that place," said the old man. He added, finally, "No one." He scratched the inside of his ear. "This summer, real estate developer, name of Deatley, he was found dead there. People disappear there all the time. Old guy disappeared snowmobiling back there a few years ago. Some hunters, too. Gone. I'm telling you. Run back where you came from. You run. Run!"

Gregory nodded and said halfheartedly, "Well, thanks for the . . . advice." He slid a few dollars across the counter. "Thanks. Here's —" The man snatched them and fed them to the cash register. As he poured a small trickle of coins into Gregory's hand, he said, "I'm warning you. Your uncle is up to his neck in something."

"Okay."

"There are terrible things in the woods."

"All right. Thanks for the Funyans!"

Gregory headed over to grab the luggage.

As the two picked up their bags, he whispered to Brian, "Well. This might be more of an adventure than we bargained for."

THREE

The two sat on the Gerenford town green, staring around at the white, boxy Victorian houses that lined the streets. Behind them, on the green, stood the monument to the town's founder. Gregory stared into the boughs of an oak tree, picking small fuzzy things off his dark blue sweater absentmindedly. Brian lay with his head resting on his suitcase, staring at the slowly darkening sky. The first stars were coming out.

Brian said, "That's . . . um . . . that's called flocculating."

"What?!?" said Gregory.

"Taking little fuzzy things off sweaters. It's called flocculating."

"Oh!" Gregory nodded.

They sat silently for a while.

It was chilly in Vermont at that time of year. A small boy with a big head went by on a trike. It took a while. They watched.

Gregory rose swiftly to his feet, looked around restlessly, then asked Brian, "Wouldn't it have been great to be the founder of this town? Just imagine this place when there weren't any houses or streets here, just the tall pines and some big rocks . . . and those." The last thing he indicated was the mountains, rising blue and distant behind the houses. "Just imagine being able to walk forever in the woods, and not ever coming to the back of a Halt'N'Buy."

A far-off clatter came to their ears. It grew steadily louder. Brian sat up and glanced quickly in the direction of the sound. "What's that?"

"I bet my adopted uncle. He, uh . . ."

At that point, an elegant horse and buggy rumbled onto the main road of Gerenford. The carriage clattered to a halt in front of the two. The driver wore a long black cape. He grinned at the boys. He tapped with his whip on the door of the carriage. The door swung open, and Uncle Max stepped out.

He was perhaps sixty or sixty-five years old. He wore striped trousers, dark spats, and a coat with tails. On his head was perched a finely rounded bowler hat. He clutched a cane. He wore a vest, a stiff collar, and a tie fastened with a gold pin. He had a beak-like nose and a walrus mustache, and his eyes were topped with shaggy white eyebrows. The eyes were diamond-hard and biting.

His manner was gruff. "Salutations," he said without a smile. "Glad you both could come." The man shook both their hands awkwardly. "Been a long time," he said.

Gregory, trying to charm, said, "Yes, sir. I think it's been about five years."

"Indeed, my boy. Five years. Prudence told me you've

15

grown into the sort of boy who doesn't make a racket." The beak-nosed man turned to the driver. "Yockly, put the luggage on the back."

Yockly, the driver, clambered down from his post. He clucked and crooned to the pawing brown steed, then scuttled over to the luggage. As Yockly fastened the two suitcases to the back of the carriage, Uncle Max said to the boys, "Won't you step into the carriage?"

Gregory muttered, " 'Said the spider to the fly.' "

They climbed in. It creaked on its springs. Uncle Max heaved himself in next to them. Gregory shoved his duffel bag to one side with his feet.

"I am just going to take the liberty of locking the doors," said Uncle Max. "It's the kind of world where sometimes if people see a carriage, they'll attempt to clamber into it."

He locked the doors and kept the keys in his hand, rattling them.

The carriage started moving.

"I envy people who can feel weather in their bones," said Uncle Max, and pulled out a knife.

Brian blinked and put his hand on the door latch.

Uncle Max raised the knife. The blade rested on the window frame. The boys saw the wood there was scored with ten or so grooves.

"Don't have the opportunity to entertain much," said Uncle Max. "We like to mark the carriage for each guest who comes." With the knife, he put two notches in the door. He said, "One for each of you. A rustic touch to remember you by."

Brian and Gregory settled back into their seats and exchanged a glance.

Soon, the party jolted past the outskirts of town. Night fell swiftly. During the ride to the house, Uncle Max was silent, and the other two followed suit. In the twilight, they caught sight of tiny roads winding through forests of pine, oak, maple, and spruce. The leaves that Mrs. Thatz had envisioned had lost their summer green. In the falling darkness they looked blue.

After half an hour or so of silence, the buggy crunched over the gravel of the driveway. Finally, it came to a halt in front of the dimly seen house. A porch, framed by thin, embellished supports, was lit by a gaslight. Otherwise, only the outline of the mansion could be seen against the navy evening sky — a complex stack of attic dormers, gables, bay windows, and towers topped with conical roofs, the tallest crowned by a jagged weathercock. The coachman, Yockly, unlocked the door to the carriage and pulled it open. Uncle Max, then Gregory, and finally Brian climbed out.

"Thus. We are here," commented Uncle Max. After a pause to look around at the darkness, he marched toward the porch. The door there opened, and the two boys caught their first sight of the butler. There were no surprises there. The dark, formal clothes. The chin, tipped up.

"Welcome home, sir. The children are here, I trust?"

"Yes, Burk. Boys," Uncle Max gestured, and the two walked over to the door. "Burk, this is my nephew, Gregory, and his traveling companion . . . ?"

"Brian Thatz, sir," Brian interjected quickly.

The butler looked unimpressed. He nodded. "Thatz?" he said. "As you wish."

"Get their luggage and put it into their rooms," the uncle ordered, striding past the butler into the foyer. As he walked in, he gruffly explained to the two friends, "I'd like you to wear knickerbockers and ties, of course. May seem rather strange, but I can't see the point of" — he gestured to Gregory's jeans — "I can't see the point of garments such as these. They're just unpleasant to look at. You appear to be some kind of tatterdemalion. There are appropriate clothes up in your rooms, to be worn in the future."

"What are knickerbockers?" Gregory asked.

"I like some curiosity in a boy," said Uncle Max, and went off down a hallway.

The foyer was large. A huge, mushroom-like seat sprouted around an octagonal pillar. A hall table stood against the far wall, supporting a picture of Uncle Max, quite obviously a few years younger, standing atop a mountain in plus fours. Everything, including the Oriental rug on the floor and the well-oiled banister on the stairs, had been perfectly restored to the state of how it might have been a little more than a hundred years before. Through an open door, Brian caught sight of a dining room where stiff, ladder-back chairs sat around a perfectly ordered table. Silver teapots and tureens glittered on the lace tablecloth. Uncle Max called out, "Prudence! Your cousin and his traveling companion are here!"

Cousin Prudence rushed in, a stiff, billowing blue dress whisking around her. A lace collar was wrapped tightly about her slender, white neck. She was young, maybe twenty-two or twenty-three. Her hair was pinned elaborately to her head.

"Hello, Gregory!" she said, giving her cousin a quick hug.

Gregory indicated his friend. "Prudence, this is Brian."

Prudence shook Brian's hand, and both said that it was nice to meet the other.

"Well," said Cousin Prudence, "I think dinner's waiting in the dining room. Why don't we all go in there and take a seat?"

Gregory nodded. "Good idea," he said.

"After you change," said Prudence.

"Do we really have to change?" asked Gregory. "I mean . . . really?"

"I wrote some instructions on how to work the collars."

Uncle Max stepped into the foyer again and indicated the dining room with his hand. "The collars can wait," he said. "We'll eat."

After the others had filed into the dining room, Uncle Max nodded to the butler, who still stood by the door.

Burk said, "I'll fetch their things."

Uncle Max frowned. "Yes. Get their things."

"From the carriage."

"During dinner, take the bags to the furnace and burn them. They won't need them."

The butler walked stiffly outside, shutting the door behind him.

Uncle Max lit a cigar and vented a cloud of smoke slowly before joining the others.

FOUR

The table was set with silver utensils. On the wall hung a large portrait of Matthias P. Grendle, Venerable Ancestor, Beloved Father, dressed in Colonial clothes and biting his own lip. The room was dark; the light of the gas lamps was swallowed by dark wooden paneling.

Daffodil, the stout, unsmiling young maid, entered with steaming platters of sliced roast beef and various cooked vegetables and soups. Her maid's uniform, deep black and antiseptic white, matched the butler's outfit precisely. She poured wine for Uncle Max, tea for Prudence, and milk for the two boys (much to Brian's dismay — milk made his face break out and irritated the webbing between his toes).

Uncle Max obviously didn't wish to speak while he ate, so all remained silent, save to ask in subdued voices for, say, the squash. Occasionally, however, Gregory's uncle would stop with his fork next to his lips and would mutter a short paragraph to himself, too quietly to be understood, before continuing with the meal. Daffodil hummed tunelessly and joylessly as she went in and out. Brian strained to hear what she was humming. He thought it might have been hymns, but it was hard to tell. It sounded like one dismal note.

After dinner, Daffodil took away the dishes, while Burk stiffly offered Uncle Max another cigar. Gregory threw Brian a quick, nervous look.

Gregory was trying to start a conversation. "So," he said. "I came up to Vermont with my parents two years ago. We went skiing."

There was a long silence.

"Ah, yes," said Uncle Max. "You've been to Vermont before."

"Yes," said Gregory. "Skiing."

Brian stared at his milk.

"Did you find it cold?" asked Uncle Max. "Some people do."

"No," said Gregory. "We all huddled in the refrigerator for warmth."

It was not a very good joke. He was nervous. No one laughed.

Prudence looked bewildered. She said, "In a refrigerator, there isn't any air."

Uncle Max lifted his fork and laid it on the edge of his empty plate. "Ah," he said. "I like humor in a boy. It's important, you know. I made a witticism once, back, must have been thirty years ago. I was in . . . where was it, Prudence?"

"Budapest, sir."

"Yes. Yes, the witticism was in Budapest. There was a man, and a building had fallen on him, and I said — how did this work? I said to him. . . . No, as I recall, he spoke first. He said. . . . First you must know, it was very hot. My company there made caulking. I had come outside, following the blast, and. . . . On second thought, it was perhaps the kind of thing where one had to be there. But you see the point: It lightened up an otherwise very nasty situation, see?"

"Yes, Uncle Max," said Gregory.

"Hmmph. Good. Yes, a bit of levity never hurt anyone. As long as one doesn't overdo it, my boy — as long as one doesn't overdo it! 'To every thing there is a season, . . . a time to weep . . . and a time to laugh,' hmm?"

Gregory sat stiffly and answered, "Yes, sir."

"Now, boy. What say you fill me in on what your father has been up to. Knew him when your uncle was alive."

"He's fine," said Gregory. "He's . . . working. At his job."

The silences between each phrase were huge and arctic.

"Excellent. Business good?"

Gregory shrugged. "I guess."

"Bully for him. Just bully."

They sat, and Brian stared at his undrunken milk.

"Well. Perhaps you two should run along to the old nursery and play a game or something, yes? Graces, or Chestnuts, or Wiggle-Me-Toe?"

"Certainly," said Gregory, trying his best to be charming.

Burk moved forward to lead them upstairs.

The two were excused, and trooped up the grand, dark staircase. They were ushered into a room that appeared to have been unused for several years. All was in perfect order. Several chairs were placed around the nursery, along with doll cradles and ancient wooden horses. China dolls and bears losing their fuzz sat on shelves, taking tea out of diminutive porcelain cups. There were paddles, and skates, and a mechanical grabbing hand, and an iron pinwheel. The butler explained that on either side of the room were doors leading into the boys' two bedrooms. After pointing out the tasseled bellpull, which would call a servant, the butler bowed quickly and stepped out.

The boys stood for a minute, looking at the shelves of worn toys. Brian approached a window seat. There was a game board open on the cushions.

He stood above it for a moment, then knelt down and squinted.

Gregory was frowning at some doll diapers.

Brian called, "Look at this, Gregory."

When the other boy inspected the game, his first reaction was noncommittal. "Oh. What about it?"

It was a traditional double-folded game board, but the drawing on it had been completely obscured by extensive water damage, leaving only a dim haze of a track and brown ripples of old ink swaying across its surface. Almost none of the original writing could be read. One corner of the game was untouched, but all it revealed was an olive green border, illustrated with sprigs of oak and pine. There was a spot marked START. It was a Victorian house, a mass of gables, turrets, and intersecting roofs. The house was painted brown, orange, and yellow. Beneath the house was an inscription reading GRENDLE MANOR. The title of the game was written in elaborate scrolling letters: THE GAME OF SUNKEN PLACES.

There were no rules.

"That's this house," said Brian.

"Hmm," said Gregory, uninterested.

"The game looks old," said Brian.

"And boring," said Gregory.

Brian asked thoughtfully, "Has this house always been in his family?"

"Strange, but, uh, no, I don't think so. I think Uncle Max just bought this house four or five years ago, just after he adopted Prudence. But that doesn't make sense, does it? This board is obviously way older than that."

Brian chewed his fingernail pensively.

Gregory shrugged. "I guess the Grendles must have always owned the house, but just, it hadn't been used for several years when they moved here. The game looks really, really old. Hey, do you smell something?"

"Hm," said Brian, inspecting the board. "Too bad we can't see more of it."

"Excuse me," said Burk, sticking his head in the door. "Do the young masters know about the chemical properties of artificial fibers?"

Brian and Gregory looked at each other.

Gregory said, "The really funny and surprising thing is, you know, we don't."

"Jesting aside," said Burk, "what one means is: Were one to burn rayon, would it be toxic?"

Brian said, "What? Rayon like clothes are made of?"

"Prob'ly toxic," said Gregory. "Most things are."

"Oh. Ah. Excuse me," said Burk again, stepping into the room. "One thing. Don't sit near the furnace vent. And you may want to crack the window," he suggested, grunting and cracking open the window.

"What's going on?" asked Brian.

"There we are, sirs," said the butler. "Right as a new-found franc. You will feel the refreshing play of the breezes. They will drive away insomnia and phthisis."

"Gee," said Gregory. "Thanks. Oh, have you seen our bags?"

"No, sir." Burk bowed and left.

The evening went on. They found some cards and played poker for a while, then war (during which they kept on making snoring noises as the tide turned). Finally, they pitched cards across the room at a doll that, when you pulled its cord, said, "My name is Ninny. I have a frightful lot of love to give."

At about nine-thirty, the butler returned. "Mr. Grendle has requested that you go downstairs and bid him good night before you retire."

Gregory looked at his watch and grumbled, "Are we retiring already? It's only nine-thirty."

"One believes," said the butler, "that such was Mr. Grendle's wish."

They were ushered down to the parlor, where large leather chairs sat around a huge, unlit fireplace. Uncle

Max sat on one of the chairs, reading some newspaper aloud in a foreign tongue. He looked up as they entered. "Yes. Good night, boys," he said simply, and turned back to his newspaper.

"Good night, Uncle Max. Oh, where is our luggage?" asked Gregory. "It wasn't up in our rooms."

"Ah," said Uncle Max. "Burk has dealt with your luggage. Good enough? Yes. Then, good night."

They were promptly ushered back upstairs, where they went to their respective rooms. The rooms were almost bare. After Brian brushed his teeth he pulled on the nightgown that had been left folded on his bed and went to look at the nursery for one last time that night. He stood, his hand resting on the door frame, and glanced over the toys as they were shrouded in shadows (for Burk had pulled shut the windows and turned down the gaslights) — the red-lipped dolls, the mechanical juggler, the iron pinwheel, the scruffy teddy bears, the wooden hobbyhorse.

His eyes came to rest on the game board. The moonlight trailed over the window seat, down onto the carpeting, and finally touched the blank board, highlighting it. Brian stared, perplexed by something he couldn't identify. Finally, he turned and closed his door.

Each of the boys had been given a candle to put by his bed and to light his gas lamp. Brian extinguished his lamp and left only the candle burning. After he read a bit (from *A Dirk on Thirty-Third Street*, Archie Temple fell for a dame named Vanilla, which was grimy, rotten luck for a private jack with a sense of fair play, a lonely heart, an

26

overbite, and a way with a .38 that made strong men see double), he fell into a deep sleep. Gregory, in his room, did similarly.

Downstairs, Uncle Max opened the front door to speak with something that waited on the porch.

In the basement, Burk stoked the fire with the last of their tube socks.

FIVE

When the two awakened, they dressed in the clothes that had been left out for them: tweed knickerbockers that came down to their knees, long socks, neckties, and stiff collars that had to be clipped onto the shirts with small studs. The collars were huge.

They went down to a silent breakfast of scrambled eggs, ham, orange juice, and oatmeal trifle, the last of which neither ate, as it looked like something that, in movies, got aggravated and depopulated space stations.

Brian found Uncle Max overwhelming. When Max asked for something — the jam, the butter — Brian tried to pass it as quickly as possible. He was too quick. The butter knife slid off the tray and fell on the floor. Uncle Max glowered at the boy. Brian said quietly, "I'm sorry. Really sorry." There was a long silence.

After Uncle Max had finished slurping a cup of black

28

coffee, he said, "I'm sure. Now. How do you both propose to spend your day?"

"Well," said Gregory, "I think we were planning on looking around the house and grounds."

Brian added, "Yes, your house is fascinating. You don't see a house like this every day!"

Max raised an eyebrow. "I see a house like this every day. This one."

"Oh, I meant in the general sense of 'you,'" explained Brian nervously.

"My boy, learn to be specific. 'To what end are vain words,' eh?"

There was an awkward silence.

"Sir," said Prudence. "Perhaps the boys would like to go and do something entertaining now. It's almost time for you to start your work."

"Ah! Ah, yes!" He sighed. "Must go up to my office. Much to do. Have a pleasant day." With that, the stern uncle rose, took his napkin off his lap, and placed it crumpled upon his crumb-littered plate. "I shall see you at lunchtime," he added, and walked off.

Prudence stared at her plate, then turned to the boys. "You'll have to excuse Uncle Max if he is a bit overblown sometimes. And I hope you aren't upset about having to wear those clothes. It makes him so much happier when people agree to them."

"It's really no problem," said Brian.

"No, not at all," said Gregory. "Except the collars. I feel like my head's on a platter." Daffodil made a loud, rasping noise. Brian watched her curiously.

Gregory jammed his finger under his collar and wriggled his hand. "Well, let's take a look around."

The two rose from the table, bid Prudence a temporary farewell, and went to look over the rest of the spectacular house.

Daffodil was washing things up in the kitchen, off the dining room. Near the entryway there was a front parlor, with books in cases and comfortable chairs near the fireplace.

As they stepped back into the dining room, they were delighted to find that one wall of the room's dark paneling had been folded away by Burk to reveal a glassed-in solarium, a greenhouse where baby's tears grew between the cracks in the moist cobblestones, and lush flowers grew around pillared busts of Roman emperors and Visigoths, all of which had their eyes chipped out.

An iron bench sat, positioned to look out of the leaded glass onto the verdant grounds of the manor. The two boys stood in the solarium, gazing across the house's lawns and dying gardens. Grassy knolls rolled down to a forest of towering pines.

"This house is incredible!" said Brian.

"Sure is," said Gregory.

They went back into the dining room, where the maid carried out the last of the dishes. They offered to help her.

She stared at them for a moment, cringed, then gave one whoop of a laugh. She turned and left.

"I guess that's no," said Gregory.

Brian opened the door to the kitchen slightly. "Are you sure?" he asked politely.

"Oh," she said, "very, very, very." She barked out another laugh.

"Hey," said Gregory, pointing over to the corner. "That the door to the basement?"

She turned and glared. "It is."

"Mind if we go poke around down there?"

"The basement? What exactly do you want with the basement?"

"Two guys with free time on their hands," said Gregory. "Why not gnaw through the plumbing?"

Brian, more conciliatory, said, "We just wondered what kind of interesting old things we could find."

Daffodil frowned. "The master would not want you poking around."

Prudence swept into the kitchen. She looked at all three of them. "Why the long faces?" she asked.

"The children were asking to go down into the basement," said Daffodil. "I told them it was not the master's wish."

"Oh, I don't see why he'd mind," said Prudence. "But I don't think you boys will find much down there. There's nothing really interesting. Just old and burnt things. And pieces of other things." She went over and opened the door for them.

"Very well, Miss Prudence," said Daffodil. She gave Gregory some matches. She said, "It's lit by gas. Remember: Fools often erupt in flame."

The staircase almost fell down when the boys walked on it. The steps creaked and groaned, rattling the old lanterns and trowels that hung from rusty nails. Gregory and Brian held candles in front of them as they felt their way down the staircase, but the darkness of the room seemed to lie upon the basement as permanently and thickly as the dust and the musty smell.

Piles of boxes and old furniture heaved out of the gloom at the motion of their candles. After the two had lit the lamps, they began to look around. They found an old hall table, an elaborate but chipped dresser adorned with carvings of nymphs and satyrs, a large lamp with a crystal case that had been broken, the backboard of a bed, and several crates of old newspapers written in some unfamiliar alphabet that looked vaguely Norse.

"Look," said Gregory. "An outhouse on wheels."

Brian pried at the door. "I think," he said, "it's a bathing machine."

"But I like the idea of the outhouse on wheels," said Gregory. "Going down hills while you're sitting on the can — now *that* would be exhilarating." He said dreamily, "I would sing 'Born Free.'"

"Only you," said Brian, smiling and shaking his head.

Inside the bathing machine was a stuffed grouse under a glass bell.

"The dust is beginning to kill me," said Gregory. "Let's get out of here."

"What language do you think those papers are in?" asked Brian.

"I don't know. Looks like Viking runes. Let's go explore something else."

"All right," said Brian. He looked around the piles of

broken and discarded things. He was sure that if they kept searching there, they'd uncover something interesting.

They headed upstairs.

Most of the second level of the house was bedrooms, so they ascended directly up to the third floor, where they found an elaborate game room. There was a huge billiard table, with a rack of cues and several sets of different billiard balls.

"I suppose," said Gregory, "we could play pool."

"I don't really like pool."

"Seeing as because you always lose."

"Okay, fine," sighed Brian. "We'll play pool."

The two lit the gas lamps that were screwed to the dark wood paneling and played a short game of pool on the billiard table. As per usual, Gregory won, although several times he came dangerously close to ripping a track in the green felt of the table.

When the game was over and the billiard cues had been replaced in their rack, Brian went to snuff one of the lights, only to notice something about the paneling — a line bordering the indented squares that was too dark to be the grain of the wood.

"Gregory! Come here!"

The other boy rushed to his side. "What?"

"It looks like this square of paneling could pull aside!" With his fingers, he attempted to pry the door open. "I can't get it," he said.

"Let the master try," said Gregory. "I haven't cut my fingernails since Christmas last year." He placed his fingers on the crack, and slowly the secret door opened. "See?" said Gregory. "Personal grooming is completely over-rated." When the door swung wide, the two found themselves looking into a small room, smaller than the average closet.

The only distinguishing feature of the tiny chamber was a window that looked out at the complicated tiled roofs of the building — a strange, angled landscape of gray.

There was a small wooden box there.

"Hmm," said Gregory. "What a useless secret room."

Brian considered. "It was probably designed as a broom closet."

Gregory leaned down and picked up the box. He bobbed it once on his fingers like a basketball and flipped the top open.

Inside was an hourglass. On the top of it was inscribed TIMER — THE GAME OF SUNKEN PLACES.

"Huh," said Gregory. "For that Grendle Manor game."

"We should ask Prudence about it," said Brian. "I wonder what the rules are."

Gregory paused, then thoughtfully strolled over to the window in the closet, a reflective expression on his face. He pressed his fingers to the glass.

"Idea?" said Brian.

"Yeah. How'd you like to explore the roof?"

"Explore the roof?"

"No, no. I said, 'Strap goats to our shoulders.' "

"You want to?"

"Strap goats to our shoulders?"

"Explore the roof."

"Brian, would I have suggested it if I didn't want to?"

"Knowing you," Brian said with a grin, "no."

Gregory struggled with the window. Finally, after he strained for a few seconds, it jerked upward with the rumble of a counterweight. A warm breeze drifted in.

Gregory said, "Hmm . . . ," then ducked his head through the window, stretched out an arm to grab a piece of tiling and, with one swift movement, darted out onto the slate tiles. "Ouch!" he exclaimed. "These are hot!"

Brian paced over to the window and, with a bit of groping and hopping, made it out.

They sat in a small valley between interconnecting roofs. The black slate shingles were hot to the touch, warmed by the sunlight. On the highest conical roof of the mansion, a mottled iron weathercock creaked as it slowly revolved. Brian stood unsteadily, balancing himself on the squat dormer he had just climbed through.

Over the peaks of the roofs, he could see the forest spread out around the mansion, the trees churning in a strong, bitter wind. The two boys, however, felt none of that wind, protected as they were in the palm of the roof. The trees were slowly changing color, especially down near the rivers and swamps, and up near the peaks of the blue-gray mountains. Spots of orange, red, and yellow speckled the greenery.

The clouds were tumbling past at a great rate.

Brian perched on the secret chamber's gable, and they

sat there on the roof for most of the morning, talking about school, people they knew, and movies they'd seen.

Brian got up finally to stretch his legs. He looked down over the lawn. The forest rose, dark and wild. There was a gazebo near the edge of it.

"Look at the statue," said Brian.

Gregory looked over his shoulder. Out in the garden stood a statue of a man in a top hat and cape. The figure was chipped in various places and had been eaten by moss. The face, from a distance, seemed bitter and hard.

"It's Uncle Max," said Gregory. "Looking like he keeps cheese and coleslaw in his long johns."

Brian thought for a moment, and then asked, "What does he do?"

"Squelches when he walks."

"Thanks," said Brian, grinning. "As a job."

"I don't know. Maybe he's the guy who makes up abbreviations for new states."

"Gregory . . . ."

"Someone has to!"

"You really don't know?"

"No, honestly. It's a little weird, isn't it?"

"The whole place is kind of strange," said Brian.

"I had this dream about it last night," said Gregory. "Odd." He turned, and leaned back on the slope of the roof. "I was at the house, then suddenly I was flown out of the house and I was looking at the mountains."

"And the mountains were covered with metal," finished Brian.

"Yes! Yes! The mountains were coated with metal!"

"I had the same dream."

"No way."

"I'm serious."

"This is just too much!"

"It's unbelievable!" Brian whispered. "Unreal!"

Gregory rubbed his chin.

Glumly, Brian said, "I bet we've been brought here for a purpose."

"Yeah," said Gregory thoughtfully. "But why wouldn't Uncle Max just tell us?"

"Maybe we're supposed to figure out what's going on. Maybe that's part of it. . . . Like we're playing a game."

"A game," repeated Gregory.

Brian pointed down toward the nursery.

"Yeah," said Gregory. He looked up, shielding his eyes in the sun. "Let's take that hourglass down and put it with the board."

They crawled back inside, picked up the timer, and headed to the nursery. The game board sat on the window seat. Gregory put the hourglass down. There was a faint inked ring in the center of the board where it looked like it could go.

"So if this is a game we're playing," said Brian, "who's the other team?"

"What do you think the rules are?" asked Gregory.

"Perhaps that's what we're supposed to find out," said Brian cryptically.

"You think it's Parcheesi or Operation?"

"I don't know."

"Hungry Hungry Hippos?"

"We need to find out if anyone's playing against us."

"And," said Gregory, "most important, how are we supposed to win?" He tapped the hourglass. He said, "If this is a game, then this should signal the beginning of play."

With that, he turned over the hourglass.

And out in the woods, a trumpet sounded. It was a high, strange note that smeared downward, losing breath.

"What was that?" asked Brian, frowning out at the trees. The mountains loomed over the forest.

Gregory lifted his hand off the hourglass.

He said quietly, "Sometimes moose have gas."

Brian was just starting to smile at Gregory's joke when he looked down at the board. He blinked through his glasses. He said, "Look. New spaces."

Gregory looked.

A path led out from the house. Space after space was labeled in the woods — places called things like THE STONY PATH, THE DARK WOOD, THE RING, and THE CLUB OF SNARTH.

Gregory scrambled down on his hands and knees and squinted across the board horizontally. "They were completely invisible last night," he said.

"Yes," whispered Brian.

"And I didn't notice them just now."

"It must be the daylight."

"Yeah," said Gregory. "The daylight." He followed the track of the path with his finger. He stood up and straightened his socks. "Let's go talk to Prudence," he suggested. "There's a lot we don't understand."

Out in the gazebo, Daffodil was standing in a drab gray shawl. She heard the dying trumpet note on the autumn air. Facing the forest, she raised her hand. She waved it once.

When she was certain she had been seen, she turned to go inside.

SIX

Prudence sat in the parlor. She sewed a fancy-work pattern onto a handkerchief. Her hand moved rhythmically and quickly across the fabric, like a well-handle pumping — as if at any moment, she would start drooling out water.

Gregory told her about the game. ". . . 'The Game of Sunken Places,'" he said. "It says 'Grendle Manor' on it, but it looks Victorian, and I always thought that Uncle Max's family was — until a few years ago when he moved out here — that Uncle Max's family was just from Boston. I thought it was an old Boston family that had fought in the Revolution and et cetera, et cetera."

She answered, "Why, yes, Mr. Grendle definitely bought the house after he adopted me. We came out here together to look at it. Oh, I was ever so excited." A thoughtful expression came over her face. "That is strange, then, about the game."

"It has the woods on it, too," said Brian. "There are

paths running through the forest, with all these names written beside them."

"Oh, the woods are lovely!" said Prudence, smiling and laying her sewing aside. "You should go on a brisk walk this afternoon."

"Yeah," said Gregory. "There's a ring of mushrooms, and a river, and a huge uprooted tree. . . ."

"It's called the Club of Snarth," said Prudence, nodding.

"That was on the board!" said Brian, excited. "How did you know that name?"

"Dreams," said Prudence. "I like to go out there on picnics on the Sabbath. But often, I just hear the names of forest places in dreams. A voice tells me." She stopped and looked at her sewing. "I completely have lost the thread of what I was —"

"Prudence," said Brian, "what kind of dreams do you —"

Uncle Max banged on the door frame behind them. "Lunch, lunch, lunch," he said. "Come along. 'The appointed time is come.' Promptness is a virtue."

"Sure is," said Gregory. "Right up there with dental hygiene."

"Glad to see you agree," said Uncle Max. He glared at Brian. "Your friend there doesn't look so sure. Doesn't speak much, does he?"

"He's shy," said Gregory protectively.

"But is he nefarious?" Uncle Max asked. He turned and walked away.

They went into the dining room.

The lunch hour, like the dinner hour of the previous night, was completely silent save for the clinking of silverware on the plates, the quiet requests, and Uncle Max's peculiar murmuring between bites. Occasionally, Daffodil would put her teeth on her lower lip and make a buzzing sound.

After Uncle Max pushed his plate away, Brian decided to ask him some of their questions. "Sir, we were looking around, and we found, well — no — we were wondering — we'd like —"

"Yes, spit it out."

"Did your family own this house before you moved here with Prudence?"

"No, indeed, my boy. When I adopted Prudence, I decided it was time to move out of the city. Too much smoke. Too much noise. People were always breaking windows. Other people, they were always fixing them. I saw this house in the newspaper and decided then and there to buy it. You remember coming out here to see the house when we bought it, Prudence?"

"Why, yes, Mr. Grendle. It looked like a wonderland."

"Indeed," said Uncle Max, leaning back in his chair.

Prudence turned to her foster father. "And the boys were wondering something about a game they found upstairs."

"What? Which?"

Gregory broke in abruptly. "We . . . uh . . . yes, we —"

"We were wondering about pool," said Brian.

"Special rules," said Gregory. "Appalachian Slant

42

Pool. The one where two of the legs on the table are sawed off."

Prudence looked at Gregory strangely, then said, "No, I meant the game you found in the nursery."

Brian said quickly, "Oh, the Let's Keep a Secret game! It looks like some kind of card game."

"With dice," said Gregory, embellishing with some enjoyment. "A dice/card game. With puppets. The hand puppets."

Slowly, Prudence nodded. "Yes," she said tentatively. "All right."

"No, my boys! I've never heard of . . . Appalachian Slant Pool, and as for the things in the nursery . . . well, I've either bought them at auctions or they were already in the drawers here. Their rules? No idea. No idea, really, children. And I don't like puppets. I really don't. Not at all. Big, goggly eyes."

"That's all right," said Gregory. "There are other games to play."

"Games. Yes. Well. Nothing wrong, I suppose, with infusing a sense of competition in young lads. To strive, my boy, is to succeed. Life is a melee. A battle. There are winners; there are losers. When a game has begun — finally begun — then you know that you are part of it, and so by its end, you shall be one or the other. The winner, the loser. The loser, the winner." He said, "Life is clamor and action. Sometimes you must show your teeth. Yes?" With his finger, he shoved his lip up like a curtain.

He said, "Sometimes, my boys, you must learn to rend."

43

✳ ✳ ✳

It was a fine afternoon for walking. The skies were vast and blue, and brilliant shafts of sunlight fell lazily through the treetops.

The boys walked up a rise. Huge boulders lay all around them, covered in moss and pines. They were on a path that wound around a hillside. Down at the bottom of the hill, there was a river. For a while, they walked without talking.

Brian had in his hand a list of all the places mentioned on the board. He read out the names as they came to them.

They passed a huge, uprooted tree that sprawled across the path and down the hill. A tangle of roots crowned the tree, looking like a nest of snakes.

"The Club of Snarth," he said.

"Snarth," said Gregory. "Great."

"So that way, to the left, leads over to the Great Cliff and something called the Petroglyph Wall. Then the ink runs out." Brian pointed straight ahead. "That way leads through the Dark Wood and on to something called Clock Corner."

They sat and rested on the massive timber.

"I keep thinking about the board changing," said Brian. "It can't just be the light."

"It could be an optical illusion," said Gregory. "Someone put out a board that looks different at different times. Some kind of trick."

"But why?" said Brian. "And who? I mean, *why*?"

"Hey, don't go yelling at me."

"I'm not yelling. I just don't understand it."

"And where's our luggage?"

"I have a bad feeling about that," said Brian.

Gregory sighed and rubbed his face. "Hurg," he said quietly.

"What was that?"

"I said, 'Hurg.'"

"Oh."

Brian leaned against the tangled roots, crossed his arms, and stared into the pines, listening to the tick of insects and the calls of birds.

Gregory stood. "It's as if we're in a dream," he said.

"Well," said Brian, "now we may be competing against someone, too."

"So we'd better get moving," said Gregory. "Toward . . . straight."

Brian nodded and pulled himself up.

They continued walking down the path.

They had reached the Dark Wood, a mass of tightly woven trees, a tangle of black-limbed, twisted trunks where the only color was the pale green scales of fungus that dotted their tiny branches. Someone had cut a tunnel through the scratchy gnarls. The two stooped and made their way through the gloomy thicket.

"Do you hear steps?" asked Brian.

Gregory paused. They looked forward and back. The floor of the strangling mass was brightened by tiny white primroses.

"Nope," said Gregory.

Brian nodded, and they kept on going. They walked

silently, stooping in the passageway, until they came to a wide, cleared patch, surrounded by the high walls of the dark, leafless foliage. A ring of red-capped mushrooms grew in the clearing, poking their way out of the dark, moss-stained turf.

"This is the Ring," said Brian.

They stood for a moment and listened to the birds.

"Gregory, listen," whispered Brian. "Now I'm sure."

"Huh?"

"Footsteps."

Gregory looked back into the tunnel.

Branches crackled behind them.

Brian plucked at his sleeve, and they sprinted forward. Through the tunnel that led away from the clearing, they could see an area where the woods cleared out and became brighter; there, on a tall stump, was the white face of a clock.

They raced toward it, emerging from the dark tunnel of twisted branches.

Brian looked behind them.

"Oh no," he gasped. He turned again and started to stumble farther into the wood. He pelted past his friend.

"What?" said Gregory.

"It's the man," Brian answered. "The man from the train."

SEVEN

They ran for their lives. They passed the clock on the tree. It read 6:54, although the time was closer to three-thirty.

The man behind them was calling, "Hey! Hey!"

They looked back. He was waving. He had on a dark overcoat. Seeing they had slowed, he paced forward. "Hey!" he said.

They stood warily.

They did not move as he came forward. His eyes were still sunken. "I want to apologize. I really do. I recognize you from the train."

Brian and Gregory stared at him.

The man held out his hand. "I'm Jack Stimple," he said.

"Uh-huh?" said Gregory.

"I'm sorry about staring," said Stimple. "I mistook you for someone else."

"Sure," said Gregory.

"I really did."

"Okay," said Gregory.

"I mistook you for someone."

Brian mustered his courage and said, "No, you didn't. You . . . you knew exactly who we were."

Jack Stimple scowled. "I have trouble telling people apart," he said. "One face. Another face. It's all flesh."

"That's your story?" said Gregory incredulously. "That's it? We can work you up something better than that."

"Gregory!" said Brian.

Jack Stimple rolled his eyes and held out his hands. "Fine! Yes. Of course I didn't mistake you on the train."

"Who are you, then?" asked Brian.

"I am here to wish you luck at the outset of the Game."

"Why?" said Gregory.

"And also, to warn you that the stakes are high. You will have to play hard." Jack Stimple stared at Brian. Reaching out and touching the knot of the boy's necktie, he said, "You are clearly the weaker and more timid of the two. So allow me to address this to you in particular." Brian shrank back from the man's touch. Stimple said, "You will be in great danger. You will see things that you will wish you had not seen. You will not know where to turn. In particular, do not trust Maximilian Grendle. I suspect, for example, that he has not told you how many people have disappeared in these woods."

"No," said Gregory. "How many?"

"I'm not sure of the exact number."

"Are we talking below five? Multiples of ten?"

"Why don't I get back to you," said Jack, somewhat tartly.

"How did they disappear?"

"'Disappear' is the wrong word, actually," said Jack. "Their remains were found."

"Tell us what's going on!" said Gregory defiantly. "What's up with the house? And these clothes? And that clock?" he said, pointing.

"The less you know, the more likely you are to survive," said Jack.

"We know about the board game," whispered Brian. "The Game of Sunken Places."

"You clearly don't know enough, Brian Thatz, or you would be home where it is safe, collecting stamps."

Gregory demanded, "Tell us the rules."

"I am not permitted to tell you anything. I'm just here to welcome you. I'm not responsible for anything that happens now." He smiled. "Good day."

He walked on into the wood. They watched him go. He walked down a short rise. There was a sea of dying gold ferns there. He passed into them, holding his hands high above the fronds and spores.

"Let's go back," said Brian.

"Scared?"

"A little."

"Yeah," said Gregory. They looked around.

Beyond Clock Corner, the path went through the Sea of Ferns and crossed a small bridge that hadn't appeared on the game board. Neither boy wanted to go any farther. They turned away and began to walk quickly.

They traced their way back past the mushroom ring and through the tunnel of close-knit trees. They passed the Club of Snarth and walked down the Stony Path.

Far ahead of them, they saw Uncle Max striding through the woods back toward the house, wearing a chesterfield coat.

They kept well behind him so he wouldn't see them.

Clouds were gathering over the mountains as they walked. It looked like, later in the evening, there might be rain.

✳ ✳ ✳

They looked at the board again, once they got back to the house.

"There's more on the board," Brian said. He rubbed his nose. "Tomorrow we have a decision to make."

"What's that?"

Brian pointed. "The path splits at the Club of Snarth. We went straight today. If we keep going that way, we go across that bridge we saw — the Troll Bridge. The other way leads us to this Petroglyph Wall."

Gregory was sprawled on the floor, putting a china doll into kung fu positions. "So what's the difference?"

"Well, for one thing, right by the Troll Bridge it says, 'DO NOT MOVE TILL YOU PLAY A RIDDLE CARD.'"

"Uh-huh?"

"And then there's a picture of a troll."

Gregory scrambled to his knees and took a look.

There, on the bridge, a menacing little cartoon troll stood. In spite of the creature's round stomach and stick-like limbs, it appeared to possess a certain wiry power. It gripped a bloody two-handed battle-ax in its claws. It had no neck, but did have a gaping mouth filled with teeth like nails that had been banged in badly. A long, pointed, cartoon-like nose protruded between bloodshot eyes. The ears were pointed, too.

Gregory sighed. "There does seem to be a picture of a troll there."

"Somehow, with everything that's been going on, I wouldn't be too surprised if there really was a troll."

"Really. Troll. Huh."

Brian traced the other route with his finger. "Or we can go down to the left, follow the Great Cliff, come to this Petroglyph Wall — which it looks like, has some kind of drawings on it — "

"Drawings, we can handle."

"Then we can go up the Narrow Path to the Chasm of Gelt. Where Gelt the Winnower stands."

"I'm not . . . I'm not familiar with Gelt the Winnower."

"It looks like he's a . . . creature of some kind. Wearing a loincloth. His body is pierced with all these cords. The square says, 'Play Riddle Card or Lose Game.' "

"What do you mean, 'pierced by cords'?"

"Maybe they're coming out of him. He looks all scratched up."

"So," said Gregory. "We have a decision to make to-morrow."

Brian nodded. "Yeah," he said. "Some kind of decision."

"Or we could separate. We could go take a look at both options and then report."

"Gregory, this could be dangerous."

"It's a game. We're competing with someone."

"We don't have to play if we don't want to."

"How do you know?"

Brian was quiet at that. He bit his lip. He said, "I guess the clock is ticking." He held up the hourglass. The sand was draining very gradually from the upper reservoir. Slowly, inexorably, it was pooling at the bottom.

"Yeah, so much for that," Gregory said, and turned it over again.

The sand didn't change course. Grain by grain, it continued to drop upward.

They watched the sand rise like bubbles.

"All right," said Gregory nervously. "Now let's go do something else."

Brian simply nodded.

For the rest of the afternoon and evening, they played pool in the game room by the light of the gas lamps while rain beat in torrents on the house and drooled down the windows. Occasionally they would look out into the darkness, where the rain stained the world charcoal gray. The woods were wide, and moved with the wind.

Brian stared out into the storm. "What do you think our dream could mean?" he asked. "About the mountains being covered with metal?"

"Who knows?" said Gregory. "But if I have it again, I

want to be going down the slope slalom in my wheeled outhouse. I want to be belting out *The Sound of Music*."

Brian thought he saw a figure break from the woods and come toward the house, but he could not be sure. It was too dark to tell.

Gregory, behind him, quietly moved the cue ball so he would have a better shot at the pocket when Brian turned around.

EIGHT

When the overcast morning sky was just turning white near the horizon, two dark silhouettes breathing steam trotted across the grassy expanse behind Grendle Manor. They were dressed in capes and flat tweed caps. They carried bags with food and supplies. The forest was purple in the gloom.

"Exploring," Uncle Max had said, meeting them on the stairs in his dressing gown before they left. "Excellent. Exploration and conquest, lads. The map in one hand, the sickle in the other hand for clearing the path, yes, the compass in another hand and the astrolabe in the . . . by Jove, exploration and conquest are what made this nation great. Where do you plan to go today?"

The boys had told him they planned to split up and explore different paths.

"It is about time," he had said. "The weak cannot hide behind the stronger. Delight in your strength. There is no joy so great as flexing one's musculature and preparing for the charges, sallies, and reversals of the hunt. Divided thus, your reconnaissance will cover more ground. Ah. My bath is ready." He had turned, about to leave, when he stopped and said, "And one final thing. Don't leave the path. It's against the rules." He opened the bathroom door. Steam drifted out.

Brian said boldly, "The — the rules for what?"

Uncle Max frowned and surveyed the boy. "Have you ever taken stock and asked yourself why you deliver all your questions in a high-pitched, strangulated sort of voice? I believe it interferes with my inner ear." Uncle Max then slammed the door after himself.

And the boys had set out for the day's exploration — Brian already looking a bit pale and shaken.

They climbed up the Stony Path. They stopped at the Club of Snarth, faced each other, and shook hands.

Then they parted, and went separate ways.

Brian ducked into the tunnel that led through the Dark Wood. Gregory headed down the rambling path that would take him to the Petroglyph Wall.

The winter birds were singing for the dawn.

Gregory walked gingerly through the gloom. The forest was dank and misty. He wished he could whistle. He had never learned how. He found it hard to pucker.

The wood was silent, except for his footsteps. He looked about him nervously, fearful of seeing some movement beyond his own.

He spied a huge stone cliff through the trees. The path led straight to it, then turned to the right. Gregory stopped momentarily and inspected the sheer stone wall.

It was about thirty feet high. Apparently, it continued for quite a ways in both directions. The browning leaves of trees could be dimly seen overhanging the cliff.

Gregory continued to the north. The cliff rambled along on his left, occasionally broken by patches of limp moss.

Abruptly, the path ended, after about ten minutes of following the cliff. There, blocking the way, sat a gigantic boulder, reaching almost to the top of the precipice. The boulder was covered with strange, spidery lines and symbols. Gregory darted forward to inspect them.

Someone had drawn hundreds of small stick figures, mostly indecipherable, upon the face of the boulder. There appeared to be no organization to the drawings; many of the stick figures walked at right angles to each other, even walked on the sides of others of their kind. Many were obviously animals. Hundreds of them scurried like ants frozen in mid-motion across the boulder. Some of them carried spears, others carried wings or cranks. Some wore elaborate hats or crowns of some kind. Some of them chased animals, while others simply walked on top of animals.

"This," remarked Gregory to himself, "is quite something."

✳ ✳ ✳

Brian walked along through the forest, his gray tweed knickerbockers and cape occasionally snagging on branches around him. Every once in a while he would halt, shuffle through a small stack of belongings in a canvas bag, and pull out a well-worn fragment of paper on which he would quickly scribble down a description of his surroundings. Crows were shouting at one another in the treetops.

By the time he reached Clock Corner, he felt a little winded and sat down, his back against the trunk of the tree. For a minute, he just watched the forest.

Past the Sea of Ferns, he could see the little bridge over the river, which the game board called the River of Time and Shadow. He watched the bridge. Nothing stirred. Leaves floated underneath it, on the black waters.

Many of the leaves on the trees had changed. Autumn was gnawing away at the forest behind Grendle Manor. Perfect formations of geese loped silently through the air.

Something, suddenly, was wrong.

He did not know what.

His back grew rigid against the trunk; his head itched to turn, as if drawn by magnetism. He shifted his eyes hastily to the right. A dim movement flickered, just out of his line of vision — a quick glimpse of an inhumanly thin, brown hand — perhaps the flicker of dark cloth against the moss. A brief, retreating thrash.

Brian leaped to his feet and, pulling the canvas bag after him, plunged into the bushes after the specter. He bounded through a blueberry bush, bumping briefly into a tree. When he dislodged his foot from the bush, the woods had fallen silent once again.

With a subdued rustle of leaves, he stood, poised to move toward any slight sound. It was impossible that anyone could flee out of hearing distance in such a short time. Someone was near him. But no one could be seen. The wood was silent.

Gregory was too far away to hear if he shouted.

Brian felt very alone.

The crows, far away, started arguing once again.

✳ ✳ ✳

Gregory found the Narrow Path tucked around the side of the Petroglyph Wall. It was steep, and wound up the cliffside.

It was indeed narrow, only wide enough for one foot at a time. He grabbed on to the protruding rocks and heaved himself up. The path turned back on itself frequently, a series of switchbacks. Slowly, he made his way up the cliff, steadying himself by clutching at saplings and roots.

His backpack swayed and slapped against his spine.

At the top, he stood and looked across the forest. Leaves and branches stretched before him like a metallic fog. He wished he could see Brian, and hoped he was okay.

Gregory turned, and saw the chasm.

✳ ✳ ✳

Brian sat. He stared back at the path. Mr. Grendle had said that it was against the rules to leave the path. He had to get back to Clock Corner. He could just see the clock. It read 3:20, even though it was more like 7:50.

Four and a half hours off.

The last time they had seen the clock, he'd noticed that it was off, too. It had said 6:50 or something, when it was really 3:30. Three hours and twenty minutes. It was off by a different amount each time. Who, he wondered, would bother to reset a clock incorrectly?

Then, again, eyes were peering at him. He froze.

Hoping to catch the hidden watcher off guard, he said, in as nonchalant a voice as he could manage, "Hello there."

No answer. He turned his head a bit to the right and, as he did so, he caught a flicker of motion in the left side of his field of vision.

He started to his feet and glanced around frantically.

Nothing moved in the shadows of the woods. All around him, the pines were still. His breathing slowed, and he rubbed his chest soothingly. He reached down and grabbed his canvas bag. He moved carefully back toward the path.

With each of his footsteps, twigs snapped. He stepped on a big stick that was concealed beneath the mat of leaves — it thrashed loudly, and he looked about wildly, sure that someone was trailing him. A nagging feeling persisted, like something was plucking at his hair, a suggestion that eyes were peering intently at him. He glanced about him and reassured himself. He ignored the feeling. In the forest, a branch would skitter down from its place, and he would whirl like a compass needle, then turn back to the path and hurry onward.

Eyes were on him. He could feel it.

He broke into a panicked run.

Gregory stood carefully on a spine of rock. Behind him was the drop-off of the cliff and the Petroglyph Wall. Just beyond his toes was a massive split in the rock, at least ten feet wide, a seismic crack that led deep down into darkness. A pine tree grew by its lip, warped and leaning out over the pit.

Gregory crouched down and peered into the shadows. He caught a glint of light.

Here and there on the granite faces there were long, snaking fibers of metal, thin as wire. Now that he looked carefully, there were ten, twelve, fifteen or so of them. They all radiated out of the chasm.

He reached down to touch one.

✳ ✳ ✳

As Brian stumbled out at Clock Corner, unsure whether to go forward or back, breathing heavily, he caught sight of someone stalking toward him, wearing black.

Brian stepped behind the tree trunk.

A voice came to him, "I see you, Thatz!"

Jack Stimple.

Brian stepped out.

Jack was wearing a top hat and a dirty overcoat. "I'm not going to eat you," he said scornfully.

"Why are you — why are you following me?" Brian demanded.

"I'm not," said Jack.

"You are. All morning. I've felt it."

Jack shrugged. "Wasn't me. I have other concerns."

"Then who was it?"

"Probably the Speculant."

Brian stopped for a moment, startled to get an answer. "Who?" he said.

"The Speculant." Jack adjusted his top hat. "Come with me," he said.

"What?"

"I'm going to take your arm," said Jack. He stepped forward and grabbed Brian near the shoulder. "Come with me. This will just take a second."

"No!" said Brian. "What? No!"

Jack was propelling him down the hill toward the Dark Wood.

"What are you doing?" asked Brian. "Mr. Stimple!"

"There are worse things than the Speculant, Mr. Thatz," said Stimple. "Come with me."

Brian started screaming for help.

"That won't do anything," said Stimple. "You're in Vermont."

Brian screamed again. He tripped and fell on the slope. Jack lifted him by his armpits. Brian tried to go limp. Jack dragged him down toward the black trees of the Dark Wood. Brian's heels left furrows in the pine needles.

"It was, perhaps, a tactical mistake," said Jack, "to wander around without your friend. You could resist more effectively and efficiently if your friend were here."

Brian was slugging Jack in the stomach, tripping along.

"See, this is just one example of the kind of strategic error that makes you highly unsuited for the Game you're playing. Stop struggling. I'm giving you advice."

He set Brian up on his feet.

"There are monsters, Brian Thatz. It's all right to be a coward."

Brian yanked himself loose and ran past Jack.

"Don't go that way," said Jack.

Brian hurtled past the clock tree.

"Come back here, Brian Thatz!" shouted Stimple, and Brian heard Stimple running after him. "Come back!"

Brian was almost down by the River of Time and Shadow. Huge faces of rock supported the mossy banks on either side. The bridge across the ravine was made of wood and stone. The river poured by below it.

Brian surveyed the bridge in front of him — and heard the footfalls behind him.

He started to run forward.

Brian heard the clunk of his foot hitting the first plank. He did not know why, but he slowed.

Jack stopped on the hillside and carefully backed off.

Brian was on the end of the bridge.

For a moment, the birds sang.

Then there was a war-like shout, bloodcurdling and almost hoarse in its ferocity. A spindly being flung itself up on the bridge from beneath. A spindly being that was squat like a kettle. A spindly being with glowing red eyes and a vast mouth of pointed teeth. A barbed tail flicked impatiently on the bridge behind it.

In its hands it clutched a massive, blood-stained battle-ax.

✳ ✳ ✳

Gregory stretched his finger toward the silver cord that snaked across the rocks.

His eye traced it back down into the crevasse.

He straightened up again.

"Ha," he said. "What do you think I am? Stupid?"

He gave one last glance into the darkness, then turned around the way he had come, and climbed down the cliff. He was headed for home.

NINE

Brian did not know what to do when faced with a troll. He tottered on the bridge.

Every nerve was hissing. He could feel his face getting paler.

His hands opened and closed. He clenched the wood of the railing.

What he thought about was the ax. What it would feel like, moving through his organs. How sharp. What it would feel like, hitting the bone with a wet thud. The bones hidden inside of him.

He thought about how things would fall out. Nothing could stop them from falling out.

The troll bent its knees and lowered its head between its gaunt shoulders. It grinned and stepped toward him.

Brian backed off the bridge.

The troll, in a rasping voice, croaked, "Give me. Give me."

"You see," called Jack, "the kind of thing with which

you have to contend? It really is too much for you. I would assert that death, really, is inevitable."

"Give me," said the troll.

"What does it want?" choked Brian.

"Your organ meats," said Jack. "I would recommend you back away farther."

Brian stepped backward unsteadily. Then, mustering his courage, Brian looked the troll in the eyes. "What do you want?" he asked.

And the troll straightened up, and recited,

"Bird of the air,
I answer the gust.
With a long, sorrowed groan
I go where I must."

Then the troll repeated, "Give me."

"The bird of the air?" said Brian.

The troll nodded.

Brian looked at Jack, who was squinting up at the sun.

Brian looked back at the bridge. The troll leaped on top of the railing, its thin arms wheeling. It teetered there for a moment, its claws flexing and unflexing around the wood, then it swung itself down into the ravine and disappeared from sight.

"Ah," said Jack. "Ah, yes. This is all a very disappointing touch. It points to a real lack of imagination on the part of those who devised the Game. The troll, the bridge, the riddle. Very unimpressive, don't you think? We've seen it all before." He started to walk away. "It makes one weary. I've walked through so many worlds. Trolls, bridges, riddles. Riddles, bridges, trolls." He shrugged.

Brian stood stock-still. His heart was starting to slow down.

Jack said, "Don't look at me like I'm trying to abduct you. I'm leaving. I just wanted to keep you out of danger. I told you before. Things are deadly here. People disappear. There are spaces between worlds in this wood. Things fall and don't stop falling. Things walk out of stumps."

Brian was still shaken. He managed to say, "What do you mean — what do you mean about worlds?"

"Mr. Thatz, this discussion isn't worth my while. Run home, tell your friend what you've seen. And tell him to stay away from the Chasm of Gelt the Winnower. Gelt moves very quickly. He's what we call *limber*. He doesn't give any second chances. In any case, Mr. Thatz, it's clearly time you headed back to Boston."

"What is the Game? Who's playing?"

"Not listening," said Jack.

"Are we playing against you?"

Jack Stimple blocked his ears. "Not listening," he said. He turned and walked away, his hands over his ears, singing, "I'm a little teapot, short and stout. This is my handle, this . . ."

But before he even finished the line, he had disappeared into the woods.

Gregory was sitting on the Club of Snarth, waiting for Brian to reappear.

"What did you find?" asked Gregory. "I found the petroglyphs. They were little drawings all over this boulder."

Brian walked over to the fallen tree and sat down heavily.

"And," said Gregory, "I found the chasm. It looks like there's some kind of trap. I didn't touch it. There's all of these thin wires."

Brian stared speechlessly at the ground.

Gregory shoved him gently. "Hey. Hey, bruiser . . . you awake? Smell the sweet rolls and chitlins, son. You see anything interesting?"

"Yeah," said Brian.

"What'd'you see?"

Brian was quiet a long time before answering. "A troll," he said.

"A troll."

"A troll," repeated Brian.

And he told the story.

✳ ✳ ✳

Later that afternoon, Brian was watching out the window when he saw Uncle Max come out of the woods. The old man was dressed in a chesterfield coat and twirling a cane at birds.

Gregory read from a list they had been making. "So our guesses about the troll's riddle go like this:

1. Not really a bird. (That would be too obvious.)
2. Probably inanimate (at least by now — otherwise it couldn't be gotten to give to the troll).
3. Something that's been around for a while, since the troll knows about it.
4. Something portable?"

Outside, the wind was picking up, and it had started to rain again. It was a prickly, dismal rain.

The nursery, however, was cozy. Lumps of coal were burning in the grate. The room was warm. Downstairs, Prudence was practicing the piano. She played some hair-raising sonata. It sounded like a riverboat captain in love.

Gregory read the list again. "Inanimate. Old. Portable. Any ideas?" he asked. "Other than my granny?" He tapped his lips with the end of the pencil.

Suddenly, Brian nodded. "Yeah. I have an idea. There was a stuffed bird in the basement. Inside that bathing machine."

"Hey . . . ," said Gregory, nodding, smiling, impressed. "Good thinking. Let's go."

They scrambled to their feet and went to the door.

Brian said, "Oh. . . . One thing. . . . Could we not split up again, okay? If we can avoid it?"

"Sure thing," said Gregory. He tapped himself on the chest. "Stick with Poppa. Poppa will protect you."

Brian stared at him. "It was a troll," Brian said. "I'm not a coward."

Gregory fiddled with the doorknob behind his back. "I didn't say you were."

"People have been . . . never mind."

"What?"

"Jack Stimple and your Uncle Max . . . they've been saying that I'm somehow . . . I don't know."

"Okay," said Gregory. "All right. I'm not saying anything. I made a joke. We'll stick together, okay?"

"People . . ."

"What?"

"Nothing."

They waited. Finally, Brian said, "Let's . . . let's go down and find the answer to that riddle."

Gregory put his hand on the doorknob and hesitated. He stared down at the lawn. There, beneath the clouds, Uncle Max was spinning in circles, looking at the mountains.

TEN

They entered the basement with the caution of archaeologists stepping into a sacred tomb. There, the two boys set to work lighting the gas lamps with the matches. Soon, three flames lit the sepulchral chamber.

The maid yelled down, "You shouldn't be in there. Poking around. You'll do yourselves a ghastly damage."

"Thank you," Brian called up to her politely.

"Just ignore her," said Gregory.

"You can't just ignore someone," said Brian.

"Watch me," said Gregory.

She slammed the door shut, up above.

They made their way to the bathing machine. Curling their fingers around the door, they yanked it open again. There was the stuffed grouse.

Carefully, Brian lifted it and hoisted it out. He laid it on a crate of china. He recited, "Bird of the air, I answer the gust. With a long, sorrowed groan, I go where I must."

Gregory lifted up the grouse. He looked at the underside. He ran his thumbs along the wood, looking for buttons or catches.

"No groaning," he said. He rattled the grouse. "Not much going, either."

Brian looked glum. "It was an idea," he said, shrugging.

"And a good one, too," said Gregory. "Don't let anyone tell you different."

They sighed and looked around the stacks of mess.

"Well?" whispered Gregory.

"We don't know what we're looking for, exactly," said Brian. "Just keep thinking of the riddle."

For ten minutes or so, they shifted crates. They found a dress with a bustle, to make a woman's rear look bigger. They found old long johns. They examined stacks of grimy dinner plates. They looked over a shipping crate that was addressed to Prudence. It was filled with little atomizers of perfume. They were labeled:

YOUNG LADIES! YOUNG LADIES!
You're no smelly APE if you use
Dr. Felix Weisenheimer's
MIRACULOUS PATENTED
DE-SCENTIFYING
PERFUME
"Guaranteed to Smell Like Nothing!"

They tried some on the back of Gregory's hand.

"Wow," Gregory said sarcastically, sniffing. "It really works. I don't smell like anything." He put it back.

"Says you," said Brian.

"Funny one," said Gregory.

They uncovered an aging nautical atlas, a 1928 prayer book, and a mattress that crawled gray with sow-beetles. There were a few dining room chairs with limbs amputated, an epaulet box filled with sandy seashells, and a jade mah-jongg set.

Gregory called, "Brian . . . here. I think we've hit pay-dirt."

Brian stepped over some snowshoes and came to his side. "What is it?"

"Some kind of a book of war photographs."

"What?"

"Here — forget the bird for a second. Look." He had one page open. "Look. Look at this."

Brian looked. It was an old book, written in a language that resembled scratches on the page. The photographic plates were black and white.

The picture Gregory pointed to was of the mountain behind the house. The sides were covered with metal.

"Bingo, huh?" said Gregory.

"Yeah," agreed Brian. "Bingo."

Gregory flipped through the other pages. There were pictures of men running through smoke and steam. There were airships with wings.

"Let's go upstairs and look through this thing," said Gregory.

"Sure."

"I think we may have some answers."

They took one last look at the grouse. Then they headed

for the steps. By the foot of the stairs there was a crate of mildew-splotched Hummel figurines.

"Yecch," said Gregory. Brian stooped to pick one up.

Little German children, wearing lederhosen, kissed while carpets of fungus crawled and devoured them.

✳ ✳ ✳

They rushed up the stairs to the kitchen with the book under Gregory's arm.

They threw open the door and turned the corner, to find Uncle Max glowering at them, his arms crossed. "Down in the basement?" he barked.

Gregory nodded. He couldn't speak.

"Ah. And did I give you permission?"

"Well, no, but we just thought, as guests —"

"Whose house is this, boy?"

Prudence interrupted. "With respect, Mr. Grendle, I can't see any harm in them looking around to find interesting gewgaws, why —"

"I did not give them permission. What if they had found some . . . some letters of a personal nature . . . or some photographs . . . or something dangerous . . . the kind of thing that punches holes in people . . . one of those things that takes off your skin . . . with the . . . the revolving . . . what . . . you see, anything!" He turned to Gregory. "You might have been in great danger, boy! Didn't think I would need to tell you — there's a Basement Lurker down there! A Basement Lurker! If those lamps had gone out, that creature would have snatched you faster than you can peel persimmons. Huge teeth. Gaping mouth! A nightmare of rapacity!"

"Uncle Max —"

"You were impertinent and rude to invade others' privacy, and you put yourself at great risk. I will not stand for such pertinacity in a relative, even an adopted one." Uncle Max frowned impressively and pointed toward Brian. "It is doubtless — yes, doubtless! — the influence of this young man here."

"Sir," Gregory protested, "Brian is the nicest —"

". . . This clever little whey-faced baggage! Whose pallor and moody silences suggest nothing so much as the physiognomy and conduct of a third-generation safe-cracker."

"Uncle Max," said Prudence, stepping to his side.

Max pointed to Gregory's hand. "What have you got there?"

Gregory held the book up limply. "A book," he said. "It's just a book of old war photographs."

"You are going to flip through it?"

"We don't know the language it's in," said Gregory.

"How will you protect it," Uncle Max asked, whisking his fingertips together, "from the oil on the pads of your fingers? How will you stop the oil from your fingertips from staining the pages with whorls?"

"The book was under a fish tank filled with dirt," said Gregory.

Uncle Max reached into his pocket and drew out some white gloves. "Use these," he said. "That book may be valuable."

74

"There were centipedes living on it."

The boys took the gloves and book and headed upstairs to their rooms.

"Sorry about that," said Gregory to Brian.

Brian shrugged uncomfortably. "What is it about me?" he asked.

"Brian," said Gregory, "don't listen. He's a guy in hundred-year-old pants who uses words no one can understand."

Brian just nodded.

"Let's look at the book," said Gregory, slapping his friend on the arm. They sat by the grate, and Gregory put on the gloves. He laid the book on his crossed legs and opened it.

Together, they began to follow the sequence of pictures.

It was a war that had been fought in the area. It was unclear when. Noblemen in wigs and long, buttoned coats made their speeches by yelling through megaphones. Ladies in long robes sat playing the harp in gardens while slugs glistened blackly all around them. Women and children in a cobbled stone square were building a flying machine out of flattened tin cans. The little girls had ribbons in their hair. The machine's wings were jagged and bat-like.

The boys found a photo of one of the soldiers. "Looks like World War One to me," said Gregory. "From the helmet. Those shallow helmets."

Brian's brow furrowed. "But look."

The soldier's ears were long and tapered.

"Hey, watch it with the pointing," said Gregory. "The pads. The whorls. Okay?"

"His ears," said Brian. "They're like an elf's."

Gregory squinted. "Huh," he said. "You're right. An elf's." He flipped another page, bewildered.

The mountains in the pictures were definitely the ones just outside the window. The boys looked up from the book to see them outlined in black against the storm. Outside, the evening was falling.

In the photos, workmen in overalls hung by ropes near long processions of rivets. On the peak of the tallest metal-plated mountain, there were battlements with scopes and guns.

In another shot, a huge sphere, perhaps twenty-five feet across, had smashed into the mountainside. It was embedded in the rock. Soldiers, tiny near its bulk, were smoking cigarettes under its shadow.

In one photo, priests knelt. In another, magicians were panicking. Photos from the top of the mountain showed distant armies spread throughout the trees, guns trained on the battlements. Smoke rose from the woods. The boys turned the page.

"And there we have the enemy," said Gregory.

It was a line of prisoners. Like the soldiers around them, they had long, pointed ears. But unlike their captors, their eyes were sunken and ringed with black.

"So what happened?" asked Brian. "Who won?"

Gregory turned more pages. No answers. Only more photos. Elfin men speaking into wall-mounted horns. Citizens of a hidden kingdom looking tired, worn, weeping.

There were stalactites high, high above their heads, and arched stone ceilings. They appeared to live under the mountain.

"Maybe the battle hasn't been decided yet," whispered Brian.

"Huh?" Gregory said.

"Maybe that's why we're playing the game."

"Meaning?"

"Maybe we represent one side."

They looked up at the game board. The hourglass was still turned upside down. Grains of sand fell slowly upward.

"How long has it been since you flipped over the hourglass the first time?"

"About a day and a half," answered Gregory gravely.

"How much of the sand do you think has dropped?"

Gregory eyed the timer. "About a fourth. Maybe a little less than a fourth."

Brian nodded. "So we have about five days left."

"Until what?"

"Until the game's over."

"Whatever that means."

"I don't think I want to be around, if we haven't won by then."

"Or if the other team — whoever they are — wins first." Gregory shut the book and lay back on the rug. He sighed. "There's no logical explanation anymore, is there?"

Brian shook his head. "We're in a world with magic."

"I didn't believe you about the troll."

Brian looked at him. "You didn't?"

"I thought there would be some explanation. Strings. Or mirrors. Latex."

"I told you, I saw him."

"What does it mean," Gregory wondered, "to be in a world with magic?"

Brian didn't say anything. He pressed his hands between his knees. "We don't know the rules anymore," he said. "We don't know what to expect."

Gregory said, "I feel like everything's teasing us. Everything's talking, and we can't hear it."

"They know something," murmured Brian. "It all makes sense to someone."

"We have a choice tomorrow," said Gregory. "Solve the troll's riddle or face the Winnower in the Chasm."

✳ ✳ ✳

They went to bed early that night. Downstairs, Prudence sewed for a while while Uncle Max read a paper in the language that looked like ancient Norse. In the kitchen, Burk and Daffodil polished silver. The radio played swing tunes and dispatches from a war long over.

Later, when everyone else had gone to bed, Burk made his rounds, extinguishing the gaslights. The embers clicked and sighed in the fireplace.

Soon the house was silent, save for the falling rain and the measured breathing of those who slumbered there.

In the early hours of the morning, the rain grew heavier. Dark, smoky clouds drifted in over the trees, giving the night sky an unearthly glow, like black light or something seen in delirium. Water flew down in torrents from the sky, scrambling down the tiles of the roof to leap headlong into brass gutters and shoot down into puddles on the ground below.

Perhaps it was the first roar of thunder that awakened Gregory. He lay in his bed, rigid with fear from a half-forgotten nightmare. A boat had been leaving . . . him lying on deck, stained with the rust . . . watching his belly pucker, and slowly form a face . . . and try to whisper to him . . . that . . .

The rain rattled down his darkened window. Wind shook the wooden frame. Gregory tried to forget what he had dreamed. He willed himself to go back to sleep, but felt only the tightness of the gut that comes from wanting too badly to fall asleep again.

He heard a distant dripping louder than the rattle of the rain. He heard the smacking of boards against one another, as if a shutter were flapping.

A gaunt and pallid hand flung itself up onto the window, groping for a hold.

Gregory didn't move.

The hand grasped the molding, and a shadowy form shot up out of the gloom, climbing the wall.

Gregory tried to breathe.

The figure climbed. A black overcoat twisted and flapped in the wind and rain. The battered top hat was crumpled on the brow. Gregory gasped. At that instant, the lightning struck again, and the brilliant illumination highlighted the hooded eyes, the stubbly chin that ran with rainwater and, finally, a serene and chilly smile. Jack Stimple peered in through the window and saw Gregory.

He raised a fist to smash the pane of glass. Gregory screamed, his voice hoarse with the intensity. Jack looked skyward, found another handhold, and pulled himself up. His legs and scuffed shoes hung for an instant in midair, then were pulled out of sight.

Brian, Prudence, and Burk all burst into the room at the same time.

"Dear me — Gregory — whatever's the matter?" Prudence asked over the crash of the rain.

"Jack Stimple . . . he's climbing the house . . ."

"Who?" said Prudence.

"Why?" demanded Brian.

"I just saw him! Jack is here!"

"Did you have a bad dream?" asked Prudence, smoothing the arm of his pajamas. "Sometimes I have one about a rhino."

"It's a man!" yelled Gregory. "Climbing the walls!"

"Burk," said Prudence, "could you look upstairs?"

Burk nodded and darted out of the room.

"Did you see where he was headed?" asked Prudence.

"The roof," said Gregory, pointing. "Up there!"

Brian mused, "What could be . . ."

"What did the man look like?" asked Prudence. "This is a man you know?"

Suddenly, Brian's eyes were wide. He hurled himself

past them, his nightgown flapping after him. "Come on!" he shouted.

"What is it, Brian?" asked Gregory.

"*Come on!*" Brian urged. "*I know what he's after!*"

He ran out of the nursery. Burk was already thudding up the steps from below, pistol in hand.

Brian tumbled up the stairs, gasping and desperate. Burk trotted after him. Brian stumbled through the dark game room to the secret door and swung it open. "In here!" Brian ordered.

Burk rushed into the secret chamber and looked around quickly, assessing the situation. Then he yanked up the window sash and leaped out into the raging night. The wind tore at his coat, making the tails snap and crack. He began to scramble up one of the roofs. Brian pulled himself through the window. His nightshirt was soaked with the torrents that poured down around him. He couldn't see, save for the glistening highlights on the slick slate shingles. A flash of lightning tore across the angry clouds, and Brian looked up at the peak of the highest tower.

There, groaning in the violent gusts of wind, was the weathercock.

With determination, Brian began to pull himself up the conical roof.

Jack Stimple burst over the edge of the roof. He reached up to claw at Brian's trailing nightshirt.

Brian swung his legs up, staring down warily at the shrouded figure in the crevasse. The hand slammed down where Brian's feet had been. Brian crawled a few more inches upward. He fumbled briefly for the peak of the tower, and finally managed to clutch the weathervane. He grasped and pulled, trembling. His face was level with the rusted ornament.

A clammy hand seized his foot and pulled.

Brian gritted his teeth and pounded on the hand with his free fist. The weathervane popped free of its setting and, with a jolt, Brian began to slide down the conical roof. He saw suddenly that he was veering sideways, about to plunge entirely off the edge.

He slammed the weathervane down on Jack Stimple's hand. Screeching, the man released the boy, rolling down the tiles into the valley between the roofs. Burk appeared over the flashing of the next roof and took aim. The thief heaved himself up and grasped the peak opposite to Burk. A shot rang out, and a tile sluggishly skittered over into the crevasse. Jack pulled himself over a dormer as another bullet smacked the roof.

For a brief second, Stimple stood outlined on the ridge of the roof, his hands raised almost in supplication to the violent storm that slashed out around them. Burk aimed once again, squinting along the barrel of the revolver. He pulled the trigger.

There was an explosion, and Jack flew off the roof, twisting and tumbling dumbly in midair.

Then, all that remained was the rushing of the wind and the pattering of the rain.

Brian slid down into the valley between roofs. He rested there for a brief second, lightly grasping the weathervane, then rose.

Burk was standing nearby. "Is the young master all well?"

"Yes. Thank you."

"What's happening?" Prudence shouted out the window.

Brian answered, "Burk shot Jack Stimple. He's down on the side of the house with the terrarium."

Prudence stepped away from the window, and the people who were gathered in the billiard room rushed out into the hall and down the steps.

"Thank you again, Burk," said Brian.

Burk said nothing, but stepped back through the window into the secret room.

ELEVEN

The woods were still draped in darkness the next morning, and the trees were coated with pulpy slime. Soaking leaves dropped off their branches with an audible plop. Everything was dark gray, brown, or black. The autumn colors were all masked by the drizzling gloom that had spread itself over the mountains.

The two boys slogged through the dripping woods, both with tweed capes over their knickerbockers. Brian's glasses were spotted with water, and his hair was wet. In his arms, he clutched a large and rusty weathervane. "What I don't understand," he said, "is how Jack could have lived after being shot and falling three stories." Gregory shrugged his shoulders. Brian continued, "Maybe he's a wizard. Or maybe that's something his race can just do."

"Maybe his sleek escape-gazelle jumped up and caught him."

"Right. But seriously."

"It's a good thing you realized what he was after."

Compliments always made Brian shy. He said, "Oh, yeah . . . I mean, no. It was, you know, just sort of obvious, when you stop and think about why he was so intent on getting up to the roof. It had to be the answer to the riddle."

"So he's our opponent in the Game."

"Yeah," said Brian. He thought for a moment, then said, "I wonder what will happen, now that he's gone."

"If he's gone."

Brian nodded. "At least we're ahead now, though. We bought ourselves some time."

They walked a little farther. Gregory said, "Now I get to see the troll."

Brian said, "I guess."

The troll was sitting on the bridge, scraping at the soles of his feet with a pumice stone. He looked up as they came down the slope toward the river. He nodded as they approached. "Fine. Good job," he said. "That wasn't so hard, was it?"

Gregory stared.

Brian walked forward and handed the weathervane to the troll, who scrambled to his feet. "You're in the lead," said the creature. He handed the weathervane back to Brian.

Brian asked, "What am I supposed to do with it?"

The troll shrugged. "I don't need a weathervane," he said. "You could give it to your friend, for one thing, if he wants to cross the bridge."

Gregory came forward. Brian handed him the weathervane.

"There we are," said the troll. "All nice and legal. You want to come in for some mulled cider and funnel cake?"

"No," said Gregory, incredulous. "You swung an ax at my friend."

"It's my job," said the troll.

"We'll — we'll take the cider," said Brian. "If we can ask a few questions."

"You don't like funnel cake?"

Gregory rolled his eyes.

They walked across the bridge and trundled down the rocky bank of the river. There, beneath the bridge, built into the struts at one end, was a door that led underground. The troll opened it and gestured. He said, "Wipe your feet."

They ducked and stepped inside.

Within the stone house was a battered iron pipestove and several high-backed leather chairs sitting around a rough wooden table. Next to the pipestove was a large stone fireplace with a pipe rack and a kettle on the mantelpiece. Around the room were scattered faded Persian rugs, books in a peculiar language, and the bones of small, unfortunate creatures. Over the door was the huge battleax, grimed with old blood.

"If you'll excuse the mess," said the troll as he shut the door behind them. "Just sit anywhere."

The two sat across from each other at the table, warily eyeing their host.

The troll explained, "I'm Kalgrash. The troll."

"I'm Brian," said Brian.

"I'm Gregory," said Gregory. "I don't believe any of this."

The troll shrugged. "I was lying about the funnel cake," he admitted. "I just wanted company."

"Maybe you shouldn't wave an ax at visitors," said Gregory.

"Nothing personal, kiddo. I received orders."

Brian leaned forward. "From who?"

"The Speculant. He said it was Time."

"Heck," said Gregory. "I don't know what I'd do if the Speculant didn't drop by every once in a while to tell me it was Time."

"You're kind of a sarcastic little fingerling, aren't you?" said the troll.

"Don't you think threatening people with an ax is a strange thing to do?"

Kalgrash slipped a kettle onto the stove and answered, "Not really. Not for a troll. It's what my parents did, and my grandparents, too. You want any squirrel in the cider? Just one? Gray?"

"No, thanks," said Brian.

Gregory shook his head. "There goes my appetite."

Brian asked, "Would you mind if we checked our game board?"

"Not at all," said the troll.

Brian pulled it out of his pack and flipped it open on the table.

Things had changed. Now the forest across the river was filled in. The path headed through a maze-like group of mounds and hillocks labeled THE TANGLED KNOLLS. There were several routes out of the maze. Brian followed each one of them. "Hey," he said, "look at this. A way underground. If we can just get through the Tangled Knolls and find this place — it has pillars and a dome — it's called Fundridge's Folly. It looks like a little Roman temple or something. There are steps from it that go underground to something called the Dark Marina."

"You like going underground?" asked Kalgrash. "You know what I think would be great? A system for harvesting potatoes from the underside. They'd grow out of the ceiling. You'd pull them down." He twiddled his hand above his head, as if unscrewing a lightbulb.

"We're trying to get into the mountain," said Brian. "We think there's a hidden kingdom there."

"Yeah, there is," said the troll. "Mum's the word. I'm not supposed to tell you anything. That would be against the Rules."

The troll poured the cider into several chipped china teacups, the kind given out as premiums by gas stations in the 1950s. He passed the drinks to the boys.

Kalgrash yanked back one of the chairs and sat down, sipping on his own cider. "So how long are you going to be in the area?"

"About another week," answered Brian.

"Oh, my! Not much time!"

"Well, we're lucky we have even that much. Most schools don't even have a fall break right now."

Gregory explained peevishly, "The only reason we're having a break at all is the cafeteria ran out of beans and dessert cubes." He turned to Brian and insisted, "We're having this conversation with a *troll. A troll!* And it's like it's with my great-aunt Betsy! 'Would you like some sugar with that?' 'Nice to see you, dearie.'"

The troll looked with concern at Gregory. He pleaded, "Look, I'm sorry about swinging my ax at your friend. Maybe that was a bad way to introduce myself. But it's my job, see?" He thought about it, and then he snickered. "And kind of fun, I have to admit. I practiced for about three days in front of the mirror, you know? Originally I was going to slaver when I spoke, but I, um, kept getting my feet all sticky. I'm sorry you didn't get the full effect of it," the troll apologized, staring into his teacup. "Hey, I could slaver a bit for you now!" he said brightly.

Brian replied quickly, "No — no thanks. Don't bother just for us."

The three of them sipped more of their spicy cider. They were a little self-conscious, now.

"What's the Speculant?" Brian asked suddenly.

"A creature," said the troll, shrugging. "He comes down from the mountain. He oversees the Game. He keeps track of who's where and tells us what to do."

"Who's 'us'?" asked Gregory.

"The rest of us."

"Do you know Gelt the Winnower?" asked Brian.

"Uck — yeah. Whoo, yeah. Wowzers. Uh-huh. Yeah, I know him. Stay away. He's a mess."

"Compared to an ax-wielding —" Gregory began.

"Compared to you —"

"Hey!" the troll interrupted him. "Hey," he said to

Brian, "what's his problem? Kiddo, if you don't have any-thing nice to say, you know? Shut your scuttle, okay? Just shut it."

There was a really awkward silence.

"We should probably be going," said Brian. "We should see what's on the other side of the bridge."

"I think you'll enjoy it," said Kalgrash. "Leave the dishes for me. Don't bother with them. Please. Don't bother with them."

They rose. The troll said, "You can leave the weather-vane by my door. On your way back, pick it up. Put it back on the roof when you get a chance. So others have a chance at crossing the bridge."

"All right," said Brian hesitantly.

Kalgrash opened the door, and the damp, cold fall air drifted in. "I'll see you later, then. Come back sometime when it's sunny out and we'll play croquet."

The two stepped out. "Yes, thank you," said Brian.

"Thanks," said Gregory.

The troll waved one more time and shut the door.

"Well," said Gregory. "Wasn't that sweet."

"You — you shouldn't be so rude," said Brian sheep-ishly.

Gregory looked at him strangely. "He's a troll," he said flatly. "Troll. You know, troll?"

Brian turned and walked up the slope.

"What?" said Gregory. They paced on in silence. Fi-nally he said, "I know, I know, he might be useful in the future."

Brian said, "There are reasons to be polite to people other than whether they'll be useful in the future."

"People?!?" said Gregory. "You mean trolls. Trrrrrrrolls."

Brian shook his head and kept on walking.

✳   ✳   ✳

Up the bank there was a line of scraggly birches, and beyond them, a field of tall grasses, muddy yellow in the murky day's half-light. A path, plastered with grimy leaves, led through the field.

They didn't talk as they crossed the field and re-entered the forest on the other side.

For a long time they wandered through the wood. Occasionally, a wind would shake a treetop and rain would patter down from the leaves before slowing and finally subsiding. Half an hour or an hour passed without them even noticing it. The sun, muffled by cloud, was only visible occasionally as a dim aura. The air was somehow heavy, and both the boys started to get headaches. They shivered as they walked. After one meets a troll in the morning, there seems very little to discuss later in the day.

Gregory muttered, "Feels like someone's cramming angry elephants into my skull."

Brian said, "Oh, really? You know how that feels, then?"

Gregory nodded. "Yeah. Happened once. On the subway, I think. Some crazy guy and his elephants. I was choking on ivory for months."

Gradually, they realized that the wood that they walked through was sloping upward. The path rose and wandered among a series of small knolls, from under which, occasionally, moss-strangled boulders peeked. The path split, and split again, leading off into branches that joined and wrapped around the knolls and parted again with annoying frequency. Gregory and Brian initially drew a careful map of their twistings and turnings, but eventually the paper became so darkened with pencil smudges and crabbed handwriting and looping arrows and question marks that Brian just sighed and shoved the paper back in his pocket. From then on, they wandered through the labyrinth of hillocks with only a vague sense of direction.

Their only landmark was the nearby mountain, rising right above them. Every once in a while, it would appear between the doused leaves in some unexpected direction.

Finally, the two took a fortunate right turn and found themselves in what they believed to be the heart of the maze of mounds. Various paths led out from between lumpy hillocks into a wide crossroads, in the center of which rose a tall, almost conical mound, heavily coated with spindly, blackish-green hemlocks. At the base of it there was an old snowmobile on its side. It looked like it had stalled there. The paint had peeled, as if it once had been on fire.

Beside it, abandoned, was a 1950s kitchen table. The legs were brown with rust.

Brian tried to climb the steep slope. He pushed his way through the stiff, prickly branches a bit, but they were thick and interwoven, an impenetrable barrier. He heard some small animal scurry through the hemlocks. Brian backed off and let the tangled branches bounce back into place. "No, we'll never get up. It's all too thickly grown."

"Hill's a strange shape," Gregory pointed out. "It isn't natural."

"It could be a huge glacial boulder or something, a huge shard of rock."

"No," said Gregory, frowning. "I think it's too regular. Did the Native Americans build mounds like that?"

Brian shrugged. "Maybe," he said.

Gregory looked around the clearing. "What does the game board say?"

Brian dropped his pack to the ground and rummaged through it. He pulled out the board. "We've been walking through the Tangled Knolls," he said. He squinted. "This is the Ceremonial Mound." He tapped the board.

"Which way should we go from here?" Gregory asked. "Which way do you think it is to that route underground?"

Brian considered, then suggested uncertainly, "Well, I'm getting hungry, and it's going to take a couple of hours to find our way home. I was thinking maybe we should head . . . you know . . ."

Gregory nodded. He said, "I don't know, I was excited when we got across the bridge. After the troll, I thought we would find something really spectacular. Maybe we should go on."

Brian said, "Okay. Whatever you want."

"Okay?"

Brian nodded.

"We have a time limit," Gregory argued.

Brian nodded again.

"You always give in," said Gregory, walking ahead. "You should argue more."

He chose a path that led, as far as they could tell, toward the dark mountain. They left behind the clearing of the black mound of hemlocks. For half an hour more they trudged up and down little insignificant vales and hills with steep sides and banks of thick roots or slimy rocks.

The day grew worse, and it appeared that the battering rains of the night before would return. A wind began to pick up in the treetops, and the upper branches began to sway beneath ominously pitchy clouds.

The two boys were on the verge of attempting to find their way back when suddenly they came out of the maze and stood in an expansive wood. Thick, tall beeches rose like uncluttered columns from some lost civilization. Covering the forest floor were dark green lilies of the valley, dead, a sea of low-lying, glossy leaves.

Far above the boys' heads, the wind stirred the trees, sending down a spray of cold water.

"The path keeps going," Gregory pointed out. The route snaked on through the pristine wood.

Brian said, "Should we turn back? It's going to rain any second. It'll probably take us a couple of hours to get back, even running."

Gregory had frozen, however. He stood perfectly still,

every muscle tensed, peering out of the corner of his eye at the path ahead of them.

Brian glanced nervously up the path, drew his cloak closer about him, and urged, "Gregory . . ."

Then he realized. The trees had ceased their swaying. A strange light had somehow drifted into the wood. The birds were silent.

A distant trumpet blustered out a brief, simple call.

Quite nearby, another trumpet answered.

Brian stumbled on the slime of leaves. Gregory went to grab his arm.

Then, suddenly, a host was upon them, a phantom host of translucent riders on stately horses, following a pack of lean, ghostly hounds. The riders were male and female, dressed strangely — some in the peaked hats and robes of the Middle Ages, others in jodhpurs and sporting jackets or frock coats and dark caps.

Brian fell to his knees.

The riders dashed unaware before the two boys, with eighteenth-century coattails flapping near wide, bejeweled capes, all the figures grinning with the thrill of the chase as they rushed after the leaping hounds in supernatural glee.

Gregory only saw the faces of the first three riders — a stunning, proud woman; a reserved, dark-haired young man in the pointed hat of an archbishop; and a smirking blond man. Other faces were indistinct, for a spirit-fog drifted between them, shrouding the pale faces and the blind eyes.

Gregory and Brian turned and ran. Their footfalls

pounded on the wet ground. A shivering, tingling fear sparked through their fingers as the two threw themselves headlong over knolls. Brian stole a glance back over his shoulder and saw the host veering away, pouring through the trees off to the right. Lightning slammed across the clouds, and abruptly rain was flung all around them. Through the mad gushing of the storm, the two heard a muffled call from a distant hunting horn, and then the water drowned out any sounds but the thumping of their feet and hearts and the hiss of their frenzied breath.

TWELVE

They're not following!" huffed Brian as he slid down another mound. "They didn't even see us."

"Let's keep things that way," said Gregory, grabbing a root and yanking himself up a rise.

They ran for several minutes as the rain dashed around them.

Then they came to a building.

Fundridge's Folly.

It was like a little Roman temple. There were no walls — just a domed roof of cracked and discolored stone supported by thick columns. The boys ran and took shelter under the roof.

They stopped and caught their breath. The rain was heavy and gray in the woods. It was soaking through their tweed. Brian leaned against a column. He was breathing heavily. The stone was wet and chilly.

Brian looked around hastily. "This is supposed to be

the entrance to the underground world. Where's the staircase?"

Gregory was looking up at the ceiling. "What is this?" he asked. The ceiling was painted a dark blue, with stars picked out in gold. The paint had flaked; the sky was cracking like alligator skin.

The floor was covered with leaves and pine needles, but a mosaic design made of little tiles could be seen underneath them.

The two looked down at their feet. They began to scuff. They kicked the leaves off the design. Gradually, it became clear.

A bat-winged, but not unattractive, god held a red horseshoe magnet, from which trailed chains of paper clips that led to other figures: a little boy in a toga who held a jar of fireflies and a globe; a god with white, shaggy brows whose forehead was lifted up on pillars like those around them, revealing the clock from Clock Corner; a fair young goddess who, draped in bright robes, carried a scepter, a harmonica, and a lump of kelp.

"Gods and goddesses?" asked Gregory.

"Or maybe allegorical figures."

"What are those?"

"Symbolic. You know, of death, or life, or hope. It was a big nineteenth-century thing, allegorical figures."

"Paper clips?"

Brian bit his lip. "No," he said. "I don't — I don't think they were a big nineteenth-century thing."

There were labels next to the figures, written in the

same wispy, alien alphabet that the boys had seen on the newspapers in the basement.

Brian and Gregory scrubbed away the wet dirt from the outer edge of the platform and found that the allegorical gods were surrounded by the signs of some unknown zodiac. They could make out a polar bear, a dodo, conjoined twins waving, and a lizard skeleton hung in a cage. They got down on their hands and knees and brushed to clear away more details.

As Gregory ran his hand lightly over the chipped surface of the mosaics, he realized that the globe in the robed child's hand was loose. It was at the center of the round floor. It looked like it would pull up easily. He quickly pulled his legs into a squatting position, wedged his fingers in the cracks on either side of the stone, and yanked.

"Brian!" he called. "I think we've found the staircase."

Brian came to his side and got down on his knees, and they pulled together. There was a clatter as the stone rose slightly then slammed down. They pulled again, and this time managed to slip their fingers beneath the stone before it could fall. They slid their fingers along one side of the rim and together tipped the capstone. It fell to the floor, rocking, leaving a dark hole where it had lain.

They peered into the darkness. Brian squinted and leaned down into the gap. An uneven stone staircase led down into some dark pit beneath the mock-temple. An unlit, evidently Victorian lantern hung on an iron hook by the steps.

Gregory was almost shaking with excitement. "This is it. We've found it. We've found the mother lode. This is big."

Brian nodded. "It could be good," he said. He fumbled in the pockets of his jacket and pulled out the box of wooden matches that they used to light the gas lamps at the house. He grabbed the rusty lantern by the handle and lit the wick. The wick was still good. Black, greasy smoke slid off the flame.

Brian gingerly placed his foot on the first step. They began to descend. They ducked their heads to avoid hitting the edge of the hole. The fire flickered across pitted stone as they left the rattle of the storm on leaves, the murky twilight, the scent of fresh rot, for the dry, blank silence of the subterranean staircase.

The steps wound around and around, steep and treacherous. No sound besides the clatter of their hard soles on stone reached their ears. Brian, in the lead, flicked his eyes around quickly in the cramped spaces, worried by the silence and the cold.

The stairs ended on what appeared to be a natural floor of rock. Brian swung the light around, and they saw that they had emerged in some small cavern. A slim, rocky bank led down to a motionless black river. The river led off in either direction through rough arches.

A small boat was bobbing near the shore — a skiff of eccentric design, with a slim, tall prow and, on the back, a complicated brass motor. Brian and Gregory backed against the rock wall and stared at the still water.

"So we look at the boat?" said Gregory.

"Sure," said Brian.

They stood there without moving.

"You go first," said Gregory.

"Why?"

"I'm thinking of the kinds of things that live on the bottom of subterranean lakes. In comic books."

"Yeah."

"With tentacles. They tend to attack barbarian heroes. You know. With something called a maw that drips ichor."

Brian nodded. He repeated, "Ichor."

"Grond the Despoiler always approaches rivers like this with a two-handed broadsword."

They stared at the water. Brian said, "Well?"

Gregory corrected himself. "Sorry. He's not called the Despoiler anymore. Not since he became king of Zolaria in issue seventy-four for feats of immense physical strength."

Brian walked forward and went to the boat.

Gregory said, "See, you could become king of Zolaria for your bravery alone. Given that you're not carrying a two-handed broadsword and your only other superpower is immense malcoordination."

Nothing attacked.

The motor was ornately fashioned, with the pistons molded to resemble ranks of elephants' heads and the valves decorated with brass vines and leaves. Ivory stops and plugs were placed here and there, highlighting the well-polished network of machinery. No obvious method presented itself for steering the skiff; the only visible control was a large lever, forged to resemble a lightning bolt.

The boat was held to the shore with two small brass chains that clipped onto hooks on the rock floor.

Tentatively, Brian stepped onto the boat.

"Careful," Gregory said, and came forward. The boat swayed from side to side, and tiny ripples wandered outward from its gunwales.

Gregory stepped in, and Brian dropped down to steady the rocking.

"This could be it," said Gregory. "This could be the way into the secret kingdom."

"Yeah," said Brian.

They inspected the motor. Gregory put his hand on the lightning bolt. "Here goes nothing," he said, and pulled down on the lever.

The engine flew into a frenzy of activity. The elephant heads jumped back and forth, their trunks sliding into tubes carved to resemble bamboo shoots. The mechanism rattled and chugged, and let forth a drizzle of stinking bluish-black smoke . . . but the boat itself didn't move in the slightest. Gregory pushed up the lever, and the engine rumbled to a halt.

Brian leaned over to examine the motor, thinking that perhaps there was a throttle somewhere left in neutral. "There's — there's no propeller," he announced. He rolled up his sleeve and stuck his thick arm into the frigid water, groping. "There's a hole there," he said. "Something where you could stick the propeller. That's it."

He sat up, his fingers aching from the cold, and pulled his sleeve back over his wet skin.

After a moment's consideration, Gregory yanked the

lever all the way down. The roar of the motor filled the cavern, but the boat showed no signs of any movement besides, perhaps, a general, sickening vibration. Gregory shut off the motor and frowned.

"Where can we find a propeller?" asked Brian.

There was no answer. They sat for a while in the rocking boat. Then they got out, steadying themselves on the side of the skiff. They stepped out onto the shore and, with a last look at the enigmatic boat, started to climb back up the steps.

In the cavern, the ripples slowly drifted from the craft's sides and gradually faded away. The boat ceased to rock, and lay silent in the cavern as the boys' footsteps grew distant and finally passed beyond hearing.

✳ ✳ ✳

They worried they would be scolded when they got back to the house for staying out in the rain. In fact, Prudence was the only one who seemed to have noticed they were gone. Uncle Max was standing in the rain himself, out on the lawn, with a hat on, leaning with both hands on his cane. Daffodil was polishing knickknacks. Burk was talking into the horn of an old-fashioned telephone, ordering freeze-dried chicken breasts in bulk.

Brian and Gregory were wet and cold. Prudence rushed around arranging for bathwater to be heated for them. Gregory was getting sick, so Brian let him go first.

Prudence poured the bathwater into the tub and asked Gregory, "Is there anything else I can get you?"

"Yeah," he said. "Aspirin the size of Mongolia'd be nice."

Prudence saw Brian on the stairs. "I'm afraid he's sick. You shouldn't have stayed out in the rain."

Brian shyly said he knew.

After dinner, Brian decided to ask about Fundridge's Folly. He turned to Uncle Max, after the hefty old gentleman had finished a discussion of some altar railings with Prudence, and asked, "Um, sir, we were wondering about that old folly out in the woods."

Uncle Max stroked his mustache, cocked one eyebrow, and raised his eyes to think. After a moment, he muttered something inaudibly and then turned to Brian. "Hmmph. Which folly is this?"

"Oh, I think it's called Fundridge's Folly. It's across the river."

"Ah . . . oh, yes. I believe I walked there once or twice. Roman sort of a thing, was it?"

"Yes, that's right. Did you see the mosaics on it?"

"Mmm, no. Don't think so. Noticed there were some, I guess, but it was dirty. Very dirty."

"I was just wondering if you knew anything about when it was built."

"Built? Oh, I'd say . . . probably the end of the last century."

Gregory sat forward and asked, "Which last century? The twentieth century or the nineteenth?"

"The last century," said Uncle Max.

Gregory insisted, "Which number century?"

"Thirty or forty years ago."

"Which would make it . . . ?"

"Don't be impertinent, boy. I know when the turn of the century was. I was there. You weren't." He said to Prudence, "I remember standing with your grandfather Cleary in his rooms in New York, all of us drinking champagne to celebrate the new century. All over the city, twelve midnight, we heard horns and buzzers. Some people had hansoms and carriages pull pots and pans. We all clapped, looking out at the lights of the city, and we all cheered, heh. I remember that. Cheering, 'Hap-py New Year! Hap-py 1904!'" The elderly gentleman leaned back in his seat, smiling faintly. Gregory coughed.

Brian pressed, "So do you think it was made before then?"

Uncle Max stared at him. "Mmm, yes. Probably. That's when those things were in vogue. Damned foolish, if you ask me — spend all that money to make a ruin." The stern man raised a finger. "'As a dog returneth to his vomit, so doth a fool return to his folly.'"

"Oh," said the freckled boy, looking down at his plate.

Gregory said, "What a great saying, Uncle Max. Maybe you could laminate that with a photo, like as an inspirational wall hanging."

That evening, Gregory only felt worse. His head hurt and his nose ran. Shortly after dinner, he vomited. He knew he would not be going out to explore any more in the morning.

They needed a propeller, anyway. They were stuck.

They spent the evening reading. Gregory asked Prudence whether she had any books he might like. She said yes, but everything in her collection was musty and nineteenth-century. They were romances with names like *Trouble in Stonking Chugly, The Primrose Void,* and *The Scarification of Azmodeus Thang.* Gregory chose *The Primrose Void.* He had not read far — the parson was calling on Miss Eggleston, perhaps with a view to a June wedding — when he fell asleep.

Brian watched from the window as Uncle Max went outside again, and this time met something tall and thin, and spoke with it. Light from the solarium lit the haze. The thing pointed with its impossibly long arms. Uncle Max laid his hand on its shoulder and tried to calm it. The thing nodded. Brian could not see its face. It wore a wide hat and a cloak. There were bumps that suggested its limbs didn't go the places they should. They shifted beneath the coat. It was thin. Terribly, terribly thin.

When it had finished speaking with Uncle Max, they bowed to each other. The thing walked outside the circle of light. It headed for the woods.

Uncle Max stared after it.

Brian stepped away from the window.

THIRTEEN

The next morning, Brian came down to breakfast without Gregory. When he informed Uncle Max of Gregory's illness, the man said, "Seems your generation's demmed sickly. Pass the eggs. Medicine" — and here the gruff man paused to chew vigorously and recite some silent verse — "it softens people." He halted to swallow, then continued, punctuating his speech with authoritative jabs of his fork. "In my day, people were hearty. Why? Because they didn't rely on medicine to stay well, no. Had to fight disease tooth and nail to stay alive. Tooth and nail! Medicine — it makes a weak race." Following this pronouncement, Uncle Max began to slash apart his eggs and mechanically devour them. Brian stared down nervously at his egg-filled plate, figuring it was not a good moment to ask for toast and explain that eggs made his chest feel fizzy.

After breakfast, they sat in the nursery and worked

out a plan. Brian wanted to explore, but he didn't want to go out alone. Gregory was feeling too sick to go along.

"We have to keep exploring," said Brian. He pointed to the hourglass. "Look at the sand."

"I'm vomiting," said Gregory. "And my head feels like it's been hit with a sandbag." He suggested, "You could ask your troll friend to go with you."

Brian agreed. He went downstairs to get ready.

When Uncle Max saw the boy dressed in a cloak and ready to go out, he approved firmly.

"Bravo, boy. About time you struck out on your own. Instead of sticking to your friend like a tapeworm in a dowager's belly. Shows you may develop spine yet."

Brian stared at Uncle Max's coat buttons. Finally he said, "Um, thanks."

So Gregory sat in the glassed-in winter garden and read *The Primrose Void,* muffled in blankets. He watched as Brian strolled away across the steaming grass toward the dark wood. Soon the gray of Brian's cloak faded into the pearly mist, and Gregory turned to the novel. Lady Blytham fell sobbing at the feet of Reverend Larkwind and professed her love; he quoted an obscure passage of Azariah and turned stoically away, his firm jaw twitching. And as the honorable reverend frantically and fiercely battled his passions, Brian wandered past the Club of Snarth, through a wood cloaked in bright, silvery fog. Shafts of sunlight illuminated columns of mist.

When Brian knocked on the door under the bridge, Kalgrash was hacking at some briars to make protective figurines. The troll dropped the bundle of thorny, brittle limbs on the table and, singing "Coming!", leaped to the door. He swung it open with a flourish.

They said hello, and Brian came in and shut the door, explaining that Gregory was feeling sick. "We were . . . uh, *I* was wondering whether you'd like to take a walk on this side of the river today. I don't want to walk alone."

"Oh, a walk! Is it a nice day?"

"It's okay. Very cold."

"Oh, no, no, no, no! Don't worry about the cold. Trolls are entirely impervious to cold — descended from the wooly mammoth. Pass me those shears, would you?"

Brian picked up the shears and handed them to the troll, who was intent on the sheaf of rattling briars. The troll sang, "Thank you!" and set about snapping twigs.

"What are you doing?" asked Brian. "Do you eat those?"

"No, no! I'm making little protective figurines. Little dolls. Out of briars."

"Oh. For what?"

"They ward away the evil spirits. Zabiminech, the Dreary One, and Mabiligol, Lord of the Stag Beetles, and so on. All them."

"Do you actually believe in evil spirits?"

"Once they chew up your bedsheets and kick over your table, you believe in them real quick. Ho, HO! Let me tell you, if I don't hang up these figurines, those spirits'll be slouching around here by noon inviting themselves over for tea, cheating at bridge, smoking up a storm, leaving the toilet seat up. Huh, HUH! No end of trouble."

"Oh," said Brian.

Kalgrash slowed his mad snipping and let the bundle slouch on the table. "Welllll . . . if I go for a walk, they won't be able to find their way in even if they do show up. If we left quickly . . . what do you think?"

"Yes, sure," Brian answered.

"Great. Hunky-dory. Ha-HA!" the troll called as he danced back through a low doorway into some other part of his warren-like house.

A few minutes later, the troll locked his door firmly and rattled the handle to ensure that it was closed. He threw a few loops of wooly scarf around his thick neck and, next to the freckled boy, ambled up the hill.

As the two walked over the bridge, Kalgrash explained, "Give 'em an inch, and they'll take an ell, those evil spirits. The only good evil spirit is a completely intoxicated evil spirit. They just curl up underneath the woodstove, then. A bit of holy water in their gin and tonics and they're out cold for days."

They crossed the Golden Field, and Kalgrash spread his spindly arms. "Would you look at this? Every color of the rainbow. Except blue. Or indigo." Lemon yellows and maize reds were singeing the trees; the vibrant shades shivered in the crisp wind.

"Oh," said Kalgrash. "I saw your friend Balerond yesterday."

"Balerond? Who's that?"

"You know him. Tall guy, dark coat, rings under the eyes, old hat, jerky sense of humor. Even more than your friend."

"You mean Jack? Jack Stimple?"

"Balerond. That's his name."

"He told us it was Jack Stimple."

"Tricky geezer, isn't he?"

"Who is he?"

"He's a representative of the Thusser Hordes."

"What? Why didn't you tell us this?"

"I don't remember you bringing up the Thusser Hordes."

"Kalgrash, we need to know what's going on. What do you know about this — this Game?"

The troll hopped from rock to rock, his scarf trailing after him. "Uhhhhhhhh, not much. Not much, really."

"You must know more than you're telling."

"Not really. I'm kind of stupid. I lived happily in my little abode where my father and my father's father lived, you know, under the bridge. Then one day this guy called the Speculant came along. He knocked on my door, we had a chat, and he explained that a game was going to be afoot and that the Thussers were on the move and that I should practice being menacing, since there was a new master up at the house. So I practiced being menacing — this must be about a year ago — and then, a few weeks ago, the Speculant turned up again and said that the game was now definitely afoot, and that I had to start jumping up and using the ax. He told me the riddle — had me memorize it — and he said people had to give me the weathervane to pass. Annnnd you did, and I let you pass, and blah blah blah, there we are."

"Oh. But who's the Speculant?"

"You'd know him if you saw him. Whoo. About eight feet tall, very skinny, wears a black cape and wide hat, has sort of a beaky nose like mine? Verrrrry ugly?"

"I've seen him! I just saw him last night! He was talking to Mr. Grendle!"

"That's him, I betcha. He gets around. He's in charge of coordinating the Game. A sort of 'man in the field.'"

"What we don't understand, though," said Brian, "is what the Game is all about, or what it's for. Or even what the rules are. There's something about a vanished civilization that used to be near here."

The troll scratched behind his ear vigorously. "Uh, I can't really help you there. I don't know much. The Speculant doesn't exactly drown you in information. I think he's embarrassed about his voice or something. Doesn't talk much. Usually just says things like, 'The Sands of Time dribble through the darkened hourglass.' 'There shall come a time when the Rules bind fast the players in bonds of Game.' That kind of thing. He's sort of strange, actually. Not the kind of guy I'd like to meet on a dark night."

Brian glanced quickly at the troll, who stared, preoccupied, off into the distance.

Brian asked, "Do you — hey — do you know the way through that labyrinth of mounds?"

"Sure. Yeah. The way through to what?"

"To something other than the Haunted Hunting Grounds and Fundridge's Folly? Some other route we might take. We're stuck, because to go farther in the direction we've started, we need a propeller."

"I don't know a thing about propellers. But I can take you to the Hill of Shadow and the Crooked Steeple."

"That would be great."

Kalgrash walked into the labyrinth and proceeded to scramble up onto one bank and then another, peering over the crests to get his bearings, then leaping down the slopes to direct Brian. After several minutes, they reached the Ceremonial Mound.

Brian noticed that Kalgrash got quieter as they neared it. Just as they were about to walk out into the clearing with the burnt Ski-doo, Kalgrash ordered, "Wait. Just a second." He snatched a thick stick from the ground and, clutching it with his knees, proceeded to wrap his scarf tightly around his eyes. Then he took the stick and began to work his way out into the clearing, beating the ground in front of him.

"What are you doing?" Brian asked.

"I can't look at the Ceremonial Mound. It's a bit painful. Tell me if I'm going the right way."

"Uh, I don't know which way is right," Brian apologized.

"Aha! That's so. Three paths to the right!"

Brian guided the troll out of the clearing. "What's wrong with the mound?"

"I don't know. A lot of the magic in these woods is all knotted and roped around it. It just hurts." He pulled the scarf off from around his head and re-looped it on his shoulders. As they walked through the maze, Brian asked, "So where does this path go, after the steeple you mentioned?"

"I don't know. I never made it all the way up the Hill of Shadow. It's quite a climb. And I was afraid of running into humans."

"Have you ever been seen by a human accidentally?"

"Nope. The only other humans I've ever seen at all have been Mr. Grendle, who occasionally crossed the bridge with that daughter of his to have picnics on the other side . . . and I've seen a poacher. There are a few others — hikers, hunters — but usually they become the hunted after a while. If they stay in too long. Things are firmer now, because of the Game, but usually there are holes all over the place. Big things moving from place to place. People falling sideways at night. You hear a shriek, and whooom! they go past you. I'll tell you, it's dangerous. A few years ago, there was a pair of hunters who stayed out . . . at one of the places that isn't safe. Clock Corner. I, um, I found them the next morning. It looked like a deli counter." The troll made a face and walked on. "There wasn't even much meat left on them. They really were only good as a soup base."

"You ate them?"

"I hate to see meat go to waste."

"You ate human beings?"

"Hey, no one else was using those remains."

For a minute, the two walked in silence.

"Sorry," said Kalgrash.

"What was it that killed them?"

"It could have been lots of things. There are all kinds of things living in here. And I wouldn't put it over the

Speculant himself. If someone was interfering with the Game."

Brian scowled as they emerged from the Tangled Knolls and started up a slope. Black trunks of pine jutted out of a sweet-smelling carpet of lurid, red-orange needles. "This must be the Hill of Shadow," Brian said. The path was steep, and Brian found himself pushing off with his palms on his knees to force himself up the hill. The troll skipped along as lightly as ever, his scarf trailing and picking up pine needles. As they walked, Kalgrash, whose television reception was poor, asked questions about the outside world. He was fascinated by airplanes and condensed milk and mail service. "Airplanes. Wow. It's hard to believe that some people take them for granted," he said. "I've always wanted to fly. I used to dream I was a bird all the time. That would be great, except it was always a penguin."

They wandered upward, talking in this vein, until they reached what appeared to be the peak of the hill. Large chunks of rock were sticking out of the garish pine needles, gripped by tree roots. And, on the highest point of the hill, where dim vistas could be seen to all sides, sat the Crooked Steeple. A large, uneven monolith rose from a clump of scabby bushes, peering over the top of the pines.

Brian exclaimed, "It must be forty or fifty feet tall!"

"Mmm," agreed Kalgrash.

"Is it natural?"

Kalgrash squinted upward and said, "Oooo, I should think so. Or maybe not. I don't know. Hey, if you look at it one-eyed, though, it looks as if it's falling toward you."

Brian shielded an eye with one hand and swiveled around. Then he dropped his hand and said, "Look. There's a house down there."

"So there is," said Kalgrash. "You're not supposed to go off the paths, though."

"It's just down there," said Brian.

"Hookay," said the troll. "But if something bad happens to you, remember I get your flank steaks."

Brian shot him a dirty look.

"Joking," said Kalgrash.

They headed down toward the house. The descent on the far side of the Hill of Shadow was rather steep. Several times, Brian found to his dismay that his attempts to dig his shoes into the soft dirt merely resulted in him scuffing the surface, sending him, supportless, bumping down the slope for several feet.

They were in an overgrown yard. The house was a dilapidated 1960s ranch, one level above ground. It was pink and blue. The vinyl siding hung loosely on the walls. Black rot was creeping from underneath the siding. The house's windows were grimy. Its sliding glass doors had been broken by rocks.

The rocks had been thrown from the inside.

Brian and Kalgrash crept around to the front of the house. A dirt road went by the drive. The bushes were growing wild. The front door was open.

Brian went to the driveway, where an early 90s–model Toyota was parked, its windows down, its seats white with mildew. He looked around the overgrown yard. The grasses were growing tall.

Kalgrash was pointing to the foil letters stuck on the mailbox. He whispered, "I can't read. What's that say?"

Brian sighed.

He answered, "Grendle."

✳ ✳ ✳

At the mansion, it was time for a cup of medicinal tea. Gregory was lying in the nursery, half-reading a book, half-considering where he could get a propeller. In *The Primrose Void*, Pobb's old school chum returned from Africa, gripped with a strange flu he'd caught from eating carrion; Lucinda heard the Selbys talking about it in the hall — she rose slowly from the pianoforte, her face still and strained. She moved to the French doors, walked like some gliding phantom across the lawn, and silently passed into the green shadows of the topiary garden. She always liked to cry under the griffin. Gregory looked up. Something was bothering him. Something he had been looking at.

He couldn't quite . . .

Aha.

There it was.

The propeller. The thing they needed for the next step toward the hidden kingdom.

It had been in front of them all along.

He dropped the book without marking his page.

He ran down the stairs. "Uncle Max," he said. "Uncle Max!"

The old man was sitting in the library, drawing diagrams in pencil.

"Tomorrow, Brian and I are going exploring underground. We're going to need provisions. We might not come back for a while."

Uncle Max stared at him.

"I'm sorry, sir. I'm sorry, but we have to."

Uncle Max rose.

Gregory tried to stop shifting from leg to leg. "I'm sorry," he said. "I didn't mean to disturb you. I didn't."

Uncle Max said, "I like this. I like this a great deal. You're not some little whimpering starveling like your friend there. No, sir. No, Gregory. When you get ill, your first thought — spelunking. Camping out. Breathing in the good, frigid air." Uncle Max strode over and hit Gregory on the shoulder. Gregory stumbled and started coughing as Uncle Max exclaimed, "No hothouse flower, you! You, boy, are a testament to our sex. I like that. I like that very much. Bully. Bully for you." He hit Gregory on the back this time. Gregory stumbled in the other direction and started coughing again.

"Burk!" hollered Uncle Max over the hacking. "Burk! Daffodil! I want packs made up! My tent! Bedrolls! Sandwiches! Water! Lanterns!" He clapped his hands once. "By goodness, bring out my old campaign chairs! You will adore these chairs, boy. Very light. Just twenty or thirty pounds each, and you can sit in peace anywhere and smoke while you survey the field of battle and watch your Johnny Rebel enemies cut down like wheat before your very eyes."

Great, thought Gregory to himself. *This is starting to sound like just the kind of picnic I want to miss.*

FOURTEEN

Brian and Kalgrash hardly dared to enter the house.

Over the whole place, there was the smell of decay. It was the wall-to-wall carpeting. It had sprouted mushrooms in the living room. They were black now, and dead with the cold. Their fragile heads were bowed down, mulching on the shag.

There was almost no furniture left. Brian and Kalgrash stared down the hallway past the living room. There were display shelves built into the wall. Something had been left on one of them and had melted, leaving thick yellow strands that drooped to the floor.

The two walked down the hall, their heels grinding on the dirt. It echoed through the empty rooms. Cables trailed out of the walls, connected to nothing. In some places, near the heaters, there were streaks of black, the outlines of easy chairs picked out in negative.

In the kitchen, the refrigerator was open, both the

cooler and the freezer sides. The refrigerator's plastic shelves were spotted with orange. It no longer hummed. Brian pushed the doors closed gently, like someone closing the eyes of the dead.

The stove had been dismantled with an ax. Huge black slices cut into the metal.

The dining room still had a table in it. Whitened by the weather, it stood near the broken sliding glass doors. Pine needles and leaves had blown in, leaving sticky white trails of sap.

The door to the basement was open. It looked like, at one point, the basement had been finished. There was old wallboard on the stairs. Kalgrash's breath was uneasy. He was sniffing the air.

They walked carefully down the steps. The basement was a mess. There was broken furniture, broken glass.

"What happened here?" Kalgrash whispered.

"I don't know," said Brian.

Their voices echoed and whispered about the rooms as they talked. Their footsteps crackled and clunked loudly on the rubbish, sending worrying sounds through all of the abandoned rooms, the closets brown with mildew, the vacant bedrooms.

Brian peered in through a doorway. The floor was carpeted. There were windows high on the wall, just above ground level. The wallpaper had big sunflowers. It looked like a girl's room.

There were smears of old blood on the rug.

"Blood," said Kalgrash.

He sniffed. "Human," he added.

That was when they heard someone walking upstairs.

Slowly and deliberately, someone was pacing from room to room.

Brian was breathing so quickly, he started to see spots. He could not stop staring at the dried puddles and swipes of gore on the rug. Kalgrash rushed to the window. He tried to force it open.

The footfalls were in the kitchen. Slowly, steadily, they approached the basement door.

Brian realized he would be fully in sight of someone on the stairs. He slipped into the bedroom behind Kalgrash. The troll was struggling with the window. It rattled in its frame, but would not budge.

The footsteps were coming down the stairs.

Brian couldn't breathe. He held his chest. He was so frightened, he couldn't even draw a breath. He sagged back against the wall.

Jack Stimple stepped in.

Brian gasped. "You're dead."

Jack pointed to the stains on the carpet. "That was where he died." Jack walked to that corner of the room and crouched down, and put his hands on the stains. "The real estate developer. Last summer. This is where they found him. The state police found him after a long search. His bones, wet and clean; his hair, of no use to anyone, clumped next to his skull; his shorts and T-shirt wrapped around them all like it was Christmas." Jack smiled. "It was not a deliberate death. He saw things he should not have seen. He went insane. He ran through the woods. It's my understanding that he found this house and hid here. He wouldn't come out and show himself. He starved. Over days. He died. Then things found him."

Brian gasped again. "You're *dead.*"

"See," said Jack, "if I were dead, I'd be moving less. That's the funny way people are, when they're dead."

"What are you?" Brian asked.

"Well done. The 'what,' not 'who.' I'm a Thusser. That won't mean anything to you. We live in mountains. But that doesn't matter right now."

"We know you're playing against us," said Brian. "In the Game."

Jack twitched his arched eyebrows. "Mr. Thatz, you should not be here. That's the point I'm trying to make. I've tried to make it clear several times. Now you see the place where the real estate developer died. This might make my argument stronger. I would recommend that you leave."

"Why? Why do you want me to leave?"

"Because I care deeply about your safety."

"You don't —"

"Also, if you leave, you forfeit. The Game is over and my people win. Everybody wins. You live, we win." He dug into his pocket. "Look. I have something for you. If you've decided to reject my offer of help, at least take this." He drew out a small glass globe. It had two chambers in it. In one, there was a yellow liquid. In the other, a blue liquid. There was writing etched all over its surface. "I am going to give you the chance to quit. If you are ever in real trouble — if it ever comes down to a life-or-death situation — throw this on the ground. The chambers will break, there will be smoke, and I'll come. I'll remove you from the Game. You'll forfeit automatically when you leave. I'll win. But you'll live."

"How does the globe work?" Brian asked suspiciously.

"Magic," said Jack. "Spells. Hocus-pocus. Alacazam."

Brian took it. "What are the Thusser Hordes?" he asked.

"I don't know what you've heard," said Jack, glaring at the troll. "Your little potbellied friend should remember that if he tells you too much, he's tampering. And if he tampers, the Speculant will get involved. Remember that, little trollkin. Any cheating, and you'll be even more mythological than you already are.

"So look at the blood," Jack continued. "Remember the danger. And run along." He waved his hands. "Run along home. Leave Maximilian Grendle's land. This isn't an adventure story for boys. Lassie is not coming to the rescue. He's not barking out instructions to the grown-ups. The grown-ups are involved in unforgivable things, and are making you their pawns.

"Think about that."

✳ ✳ ✳

Gregory was playing chess with Prudence in the sitting room when Brian returned. A fire burned in the hearth; Brian had seen its hazy smoke trailing above the brittle leaves from a ways off. He had run toward the house and burst in, short of breath.

"Did you have a nice walk?" asked Prudence.

"It was surprising," said Brian. "Gregory, could I talk to you?"

"It sounds nice," said Prudence as she moved her queen nimbly out of the way of Gregory's impatient bishop.

"What did you find?" asked Gregory.

"A house," said Brian, looking carefully at Prudence. "A house near a steeple of stone."

"What?" said Gregory, turning back to the board.

Brian was impatient. He started to go upstairs.

"Will you excuse me?" Gregory said to his cousin. "It looks like someone has his underwear in a twist."

Brian was up on the landing. Gregory followed, gloating, "You'll never guess what I found today."

"Listen —"

"No, you listen. Guess what I found!" They entered the nursery.

"What?"

"I realized it earlier today, as I was sitting in here . . . well, trying to get a particularly big chunk out of my nostril or whatever."

"What?"

"Look around, my friend! See a propeller appear before your very eyes!"

Brian surveyed the room eagerly. China dolls were slumped on shelves. Teddy bears dangled threadbare arms. A hand-knit clown drooped onto a red-lipped sock monkey. Suddenly, the dark-haired boy cried softly, "The iron pinwheel!"

"Yup. Stick the stick into the socket on the motor and the propeller part will be in just the right position."

"Brilliant!" Brian commended.

"Thanks. I've had Uncle Max set us up with backpacks and provisions. Sick or well, I don't care. We don't have time. No time for hurling. Tomorrow, we'll be on our way down the underground river."

They sat then and talked about what Brian had found that day.

Brian told him about the house, right down to Jack Stimple telling them Lassie wouldn't come to their rescue.

"I don't know what it means," Brian concluded, pacing.

"I know what it means," Gregory said. "It means that jerk has Lassie tied up somewhere. It means our dear, precious little varmint is — "

"Will you stop joking?" Brian said. "Would you — I'm sorry. Would you just stop it."

"I can't stop. I can't stop it," Gregory said miserably. He lay down and put his arm over his eyes. "I keep on thinking of jokes right now. I'm thinking of them faster and faster. All about Lassie."

"We have to do something," said Brian.

"I know," said Gregory. "I know, I know, I know."

"We're in danger!"

Gregory was stunned. He said, "Hey. You shouted at me."

Brian looked down. He said, "I'm sorry."

"I don't think you've ever yelled at me."

"It's just — sometimes you get — you know. . . . Sometimes things aren't funny."

Gregory said quietly, "No. Sometimes they aren't." The he looked out the window. He said. "What will we do? What will we do, what will we do?"

Brian said, "I don't know."

And Gregory said, "It's almost time for dinner."

❋ ❋ ❋

The silence of the dinner hour was filled with the bumpings and muffled rattlings of the wind outside the house. Through the dark panes of the winter garden's glass, the trees could be seen, flinging from side to side against the incandescent blue night. Occasionally, the wind would whip through some grotto and yowl like an angered cat, and everyone would carefully look up from their food, then look down again as the keening faded away. The tapping of silver against china, the whispers of requests for second helpings, and the burbling of water into goblets were the only sounds to be heard, besides the wind's angry shrieks and thumps.

Gregory announced loudly, "Brian found your house today."

Uncle Max said, "I don't believe in speech during the supper hour. It interferes with digestion."

Gregory said, "He found your house. Your real house."

126

He let this sink in. Then he added, "The house where Prudence lived in a room downstairs with sunflower wallpaper."

Uncle Max turned to Brian. "Where did you find this . . . *house?*"

Brian answered, low in his seat, "Near the . . . near the Crooked Steeple."

Uncle Max glared at the boy. "Boy. Did you go off the path?"

"Yes, sir."

"You left the paths?"

Brian simply nodded, his already pale face turning paler.

Uncle Max rose darkly, his beak-like nose turning scarlet. "I told you never — NEVER! — to go off the paths, didn't I?"

Brian nodded.

"You FOOL!" shouted Uncle Max.

Prudence flinched, but then, in a quavering voice, said, "What . . . why?"

The man turned to her. "What do you mean?" he snapped.

"I asked why they can't go off the paths. I've gone off the paths —"

"Because I said so. IS THAT NOT SUFFICIENT REASON?" He glared around wildly. "AM I NOT MASTER IN THIS HOUSE?" he shouted. "I AM MASTER! IT IS FOR ME TO DICTATE WHAT OTHERS DO! IS THIS UNDERSTOOD?"

Prudence looked down at her lap and touched her fingers skittishly to her face, a dark blush spreading across her smooth cheeks. Brian bit his lower lip and stared at the candelabra.

Gregory rose. "I think you owe us an explanation, sir."

Uncle Max turned hotly toward his foster-nephew. He hissed, "What?"

"I think you owe us an explanation. You have obviously brought us here for some purpose, for some strange game, and it's time we found out the rules. It's time we found out what we're playing for."

Uncle Max's eyes were wide and white. His face was scarlet.

"Our lives have been in danger, sir, as a result of this game. Something has stalked us out in the woods. Jack Stimple tried to kill Brian on the roof that night. If we're going to play your game, we demand to know the rules."

Uncle Max merely stared, incredulous, at his nephew.

Prudence looked up timidly and said quietly, "Yes. What IS going on?"

Brian added, "We . . . we need to understand how and why all of this is here."

Uncle Max stared at the floor, whispering silently to himself. Prudence could not bear to look at him, but ducked her head, almost crying.

Rubbing his mustache, he turned to the wall and quietly said, "All right. You'll hear about it. In the parlor. Burk — coffee, tea, and dessert in the parlor."

"Very good, sir."

"After we finish our meal."

He kept eating in silence. His eyes were almost closed. The others watched him as they ate. He put far too much beef between his lips. His cheeks bulged. He gnawed for a long time and jerked his head as he swallowed.

It took them ten minutes to finish.

FIFTEEN

Uncle Max strolled through the foyer into the parlor, then sat resolutely in one of the wing-back chairs by the fire. He wearily caressed his temple with one heavy hand, continually muttering to himself.

The others shuffled in, looking stiff and nervous. They arranged themselves in various seats around the room. Burk brought in a tray with tea, coffee, and napoleons, which he distributed quietly. The fire popped and snapped in the hearth, while outside the wind battered the slats of the great house.

Uncle Max looked up. "You want me to explain. Suppose I like that in a boy — enough gumption to stand up for his right to understand. I'll tell you. It'll be breaking the Rules, but —" He nodded.

They waited. Brian was sitting on his hands. Gregory plucked at the fabric of his pants.

"What do you know?" asked Uncle Max.

"Not much," said Brian.

"Enough," Gregory said. "Brian and I are playing a game against someone named Jack Stimple, whose real name is Balerond. He's part of something called the Thusser Hordes. Years ago, there was a big battle."

"There was," Uncle Max confirmed.

"The Thusser Hordes were fighting some kind of elfin people who live inside the mountains. The game we're playing, the Game of Sunken Places — it has something to do with that battle."

"Indeed," said Uncle Max.

"What does it have to do with the battle?"

"Two parties are betting on the outcome."

"Who's betting?"

"The Thusser Hordes and the People of the Mound of Norumbega."

"Who are they?" asked Brian.

Uncle Max just blinked at the paneling, looking over the boys' heads.

"Who . . . ?" Brian began again, but Uncle Max did not move. Prudence cleared her throat.

Gregory tried, "And if we win?"

"Who," asked Uncle Max, "is 'we'?" He drank his coffee, then sat back in his chair. He said, "Two spirit-nations are at war. You will decide the conflict. On the one side, there are the People of the Mound of Norumbega, who used to live here. On the other side, the Thusser Hordes, who drove them out." Uncle Max bowed his head against the headrest of the chair.

Gregory demanded, "What happens if we lose?"

"A treaty was struck," said Uncle Max. "The People of Norumbega were forced into exile. But there is a chance for return. The Game is arranged. Rounds are played. If the Norumbegans win, they will return from their exile. If the Thusser Hordes win, they will take possession of the mountain, the Mound of Norumbega."

Brian was incredulous. "The fate of this whole spirit-nation depends on whether we win or lose?"

"I would appreciate it if you gave it your one hundred percent."

"But if we don't win," Brian said, "the People of Norumbega will be exiled forever?"

Gregory protested, "What kind of people would risk their whole nation on a game? Especially a game played by us?"

"A spirit-people for whom there is nothing but play," Max answered. "An enchanted people for whom even their own pain is an entertainment. A people who do not know right and wrong, who breathe an air that is thinner than ours, without the dust and skin of our thick, sublunary atmosphere."

"So who are you?" asked Gregory. "Why do you know this?"

Max considered. "When I was a child," he said, "which was . . ." He stopped and he held up a finger. "What was that?" he whispered.

There was a ticking all around them. A deep, heavy ticking, as if water were dripping on a distant drum and picking up speed, dripping ever faster and faster and louder until it filled the room and was no longer a ticking but — abruptly, there was a tremendous roaring hiss outside, and everyone started up out of their chairs. Darkness shot through the house — the flames were squelched. All around them thundered a great rumbling. Daffodil, in the kitchen, screamed in the darkness. The front door slammed open, and wind and leaves burst through the house. The murky forms of the panicked group ran to and fro.

Huge, dark wings were beating around the house.

Over the din, Uncle Max shouted, "IT'S THE THUSSER HORDES! I'VE TOLD YOU TOO MUCH! GO! GET OUT OF THE HOUSE!"

Gregory and Brian looked at each other, frantic. Brian scrambled to the steps and began to stumble upward, though great suckings and buffetings of wind slammed around him, and darkness and shadows writhed all about. He fell into the nursery and snatched the pinwheel, which slowly turned in the breeze. A doll, knocked by his grab, toppled to the floor and landed sluggishly on its shoulder.

Brian flew back out onto the landing and began to charge down the steps. From above, on the stairs descending from the game room, countless tiny feet were rattling down the steps, bearing sinuous, strange bodies. Dark things ran and shouted through the house, and lurked in the rooms and the peaked roofs. And all around, outside, one great monstrosity flapped great dark wings.

Gregory stood by the door, two backpacks slung over his shoulder. Uncle Max ran out of the parlor as Brian landed on the floor, still clutching the propeller. The old man pointed ferociously to the door and ordered, "RUN! GO! GET OUT!"

"What about Prudence?" Gregory demanded. "What about her?"

"She's not going," said Uncle Max. "She's safer here. She's not playing."

"Prudence!" shouted Gregory.

"I'll hold her here! She is not playing!" Uncle Max insisted. "She will be safe once you leave!"

The door stood open. The wind howled around. Gregory and Brian ran out into the storm. The wind roared all around them. Within the windows of the house, they saw strange glowing eyes, and saw quick movements leaping across the rooftop, spiked spines against the sky.

Into the forest they plunged, and around them the leaves were alive with chitterings and calls in the gale, and the trees rocked, and hoarse throats howled, and in the night, countless strange things gibbered.

✳ ✳ ✳

Things passed in herds.

The boys could tell that doors were opened.

Down a ravine, there was no forest floor.

They ran past it. There was a hole.

Brian scrambled to catch up with Gregory.

Gregory was not waiting for him.

Something was thrashing in the leaves.

They reached the Club of Snarth.

Then, in the trees, there was a calling. Gregory stepped sideways and crouched behind a rhododendron large as a bear. Brian almost ran past him.

Gregory grabbed his friend — and they both froze.

Gelt the Winnower swung through the trees above them.

The boys, in half-squats, did not move — but stared.

He was like a man in form, though strangely altered, with spikes driven through his limbs; where each spike went in, a thin silver wire snaked out — and the wires whipped and swung through the treetops, prodding and clutching, nudging — some of them hung down through dead branches like tickling winter rains.

"Don't move," whispered Gregory. Carefully, he lifted wet branches and stretched them over their heads.

The wires glided toward them, tapping across the leaves that lay on the ground.

Above them, the Winnower gripped treetrops and swung his gaunt head from side to side. His eyes were wide and white, and glistened as they peered through the wood.

The filaments brushed across saplings and toward Brian's shoes. His ankles were turned where he crouched. His socks were wet.

Gregory flinched — a wire was scraping across the branch in his hand. Now another. It flicked the leaves and licked their stems almost tenderly.

Brian saw two more wires headed toward him, snaking through the air, curling and uncurling.

And then they heard something else on the path.

Hoofbeats.

The filaments lifted. The Winnower crouched in the sky.

An old black automobile, chrome shining, was being dragged through the forest by a team of white horses.

Gregory and Brian slithered closer to their rhododendron.

The car drew up near them. It was heading for the mansion. A passenger door opened, and a man climbed out. In the half-light he looked like Jack Stimple — the dark, ringed eyes, the long, dark coat. He wore a homburg hat and smoked a cigar. But his voice, when he called up to Gelt, was not Jack's. He spoke in an alien tongue.

Gelt called back down to him in chirps and twitters.

The man nodded and stepped back into the car.

The horses began dragging the car again through the haunted wood.

Up in the trees, Gelt followed.

They headed for the house.

When they were gone, Brian and Gregory rose from the bushes.

They darted breathlessly into the Dark Wood. The spiky branches sawed around them in the wind.

Somewhere, there was a sound like jets and geysers.

And everywhere, things were howling and moving.

☀ PART TWO ☀

SIXTEEN

Kalgrash was seated in his cramped, warm library, *A Child's Picture-Book of Giddy Heroes* lying open on his lap, when he heard a frantic pounding from upstairs. He slid the heavy volume off his knees and left it open on the cracked leather chair, then bounced up a steep set of steps, through a dank stone hall, and into his kitchen. Someone was thumping violently on the front door.

The troll plucked a few amulets from where they were sprawled on the table and held them warily forward as he unlocked the door. When it opened, however, he was confronted by no horde of evil spirits but, instead, merely Brian and Gregory, both hunched and shivering in their coats, each clutching an overstuffed pack.

"Why, hello!" exclaimed the troll. "Ha-HA! Guests at this time of night! Nifty!" He crowed, "Come in, come in, come in! We'll sit by the fire! We'll eat some toasted cheese sandwiches! We can play Scrabble. Remember, I can't read and I'm fond of made-up words with no vowels."

Gregory stepped in, and Brian quickly said, "We may be being followed by something."

"Oh, dear! And you're wet, wet, wet! Take off your coats! Sit down by the fire! Let me get you some mulled wine. . . ."

Brian stepped in and swiftly shut the door behind him.

Gregory threw back his shoulders, and his tweed coat slumped off down his arms. The boys appeared pale, even in the ruddy light from the woodstove, and their hair hung in thick hummocks. Their feet and lower legs were soaking wet.

"Dear, dear, dear! What . . . what happened?" asked the troll, concerned, as he slammed the kettle down on the woodstove.

Both started to talk simultaneously; Brian deferred. Gregory explained, "We . . . we were chased out of Uncle Max's house. He finally started to tell us about what was going on, and then this huge thing came and surrounded the house. Uncle Max told us to run for our lives and, um, we did. But there were all sorts of strange things in the woods. . . ."

"We heard all sorts of strange noises," Brian said, his voice husky and grainy. He dipped his head and forcefully cleared his throat, then continued: "There were these huge things moving around. . . . They were about seven feet tall, with sort of huge humped backs. . . . that's all we could see. And something was flying overhead."

Gregory said, "We saw Gelt the Winnower."

Kalgrash turned his head, standing before the stove. "Maximilian Grendle was about to give away the Game?" he asked.

"Yes," answered Brian. "He had just started to when this thing attacked."

Kalgrash scowled briefly, the thin fingers of one hand lightly resting on the wicker handle of the teapot. "It doesn't seem likely. To forfeit the Game . . . dear, dear, dear."

Kalgrash peered around, attempting to locate some mugs. "I'm, uh, afraid that all of my cups were smashed by Galagazol the Wide and Impertinent One. You won't mind using bowls, will you?"

Both boys said no, and the troll set about rummaging through a pile of rabbit skins and bundles of herbs. "Uh, I guess plates wouldn't do the trick, would they, no. . . ." he mused. At length, he pulled out a bowl and a cup and carefully filled them with dark mulled wine. "Here, come down to the library. I was just reading *A Child's Picture-Book of Giddy Heroes*. Well, um, looking at the pictures, actually. There's a really keen one of Prince Lorenzi petrified with fear of heights near the Great Gap of Ben-Droobi. You can practically see him shaking on his camel." The squat troll shuffled down the creaking staircase.

The tiny library was comfortably warm — there was a small fireplace with a cracked wooden mantel carved to resemble a chorus of runny-nosed imps. Books were stacked haphazardly on crooked shelves between strips of

141

oak paneling. A dark portrait of a troll in a seventeenth-century ruff hung in the shadows above the fireplace. "Sit down," offered Kalgrash. "Take a seat. There are some blankets there. Wrap up warmly or you'll both be sick, sick, sick. Retching like it was going out of style." Suddenly, the troll stopped to consider. "That's a sort of strange idea, isn't it, retching like it was going out of style. Imagine if it were in style."

They wrapped the wool blankets around their shoulders and huddled by the fire, Gregory leaning against the arm of the leather chair. Kalgrash resumed his perch and picked up his book, setting it on his spiky knees. "Do you want me to tell you some of the stories from this book? I can remember JUST how my father told them to me."

"Sure," said Gregory. Brian nodded.

"Hmm. I was just getting to the pictures for 'The Tale of Sir Roland, Acrophobic Duke of Aquitaine. . . .'"

Kalgrash's inhuman voice prattled on happily, affecting deep, booming tones or high-pitched, Southern-accented ones as the needs of the stories dictated. The two boys sipped their mulled wine silently and stared at where the troll sat with his head inclined backward on the yellow-stained lace doily. Dim stories passed through their ears of monks who fled the Deepest Pits of Hell in favor of the Shallower Pits of Hell, of Hannibal's warriors who opted out of riding elephants through the Alps in favor of invading via the lowlands on tortoise-back. Gradually, the two grew tired, and their heads began nodding against the rough, tickly wool of the blankets. As the fire quietly sighed, they fell to sleep entirely, the echoes of

Kalgrash's voice forming strange landscapes in their dreams.

✳ ✳ ✳

They woke; the fire was mere orange embers. Kalgrash was gone. A frigid wind pattered through the room. Brian rose, dropping the stiff blanket from around him. He stormed up the creaking stairs and yelped from the kitchen. Gregory raced after him.

The thick door to the outside was wide open, and leaves and rain blew in. The table was thrown on its side. Litter was strewn across the hearth and chairs and cabinets — bones and pelts and broken crockery. On the floor, twitching and grumbling, Kalgrash lay in convulsions. "Bitty, bitty, bitty," he dribbled. "Deeth, deeth . . . kark, no, no, but don't come again . . . no, go away go away tell them to go away!"

"What's . . . what's wrong?" Brian asked timidly.

"Kreek, kreek . . . but no bye-bye . . . trith dribble." He flung his head left and right, blinking blindly.

Brian called, "Kalgrash!" but the troll stared dimly into space and slapped his arms back and forth wildly.

"They're here! They're here!" The troll kicked fiercely with his foot, and a tin of buttons and thread upset with a clatter.

Brian stepped over the overturned table and scattered chairs, the wind throwing back his hair. He slammed shut the door. Kalgrash jerked at the noise.

There was a brief period of silence, where only the

mythical beast's muttering could be heard. Shakily, the troll's gaunt hand reached for an amulet that lay on the floor. Suddenly, he snatched it, gave a shout of, "Ah-HA!" and collapsed entirely into snoring slumber.

The two stood numbly, looking around at the wreckage.

Outside, the wind played about the bridge and forced the river to tumble along at a reckless pace. Inside the troll's house, Gregory stoked the fires as gray morning drew near.

✳   ✳   ✳

Brian's yelp awakened the troll; the boy had been frightened by the scuttling lizard that lived in a woolen stocking cap beneath the woodpile. Kalgrash lay with open eyes, staring at the fire. Suddenly, he leaped to his feet. "GOOD morning!" he sang, grinning widely. Gregory had been slumbering in the chair next to the troll — he looked up groggily, slowly blinking.

"Oh, good morning," Gregory said.

"Omelettes for breakfast?" suggested the troll, rubbing his spindly hands together vigorously.

"Oh. Sure. Brian loves eggs," Gregory agreed. "And a big glass of milk."

"Splendid!" And the troll threw up his hands and bounded up the staircase, down the hallway, and into the kitchen. Brian called from the basement, "I think there's something living beneath the woodpile."

The troll shuffled halfway down the hallway to the

144

basement steps. "Oh, yes, yes, yes, yes . . . I think it eats dried pasta. All of my egg noodles keep disappearing."

"What should I do?"

"Fish around with your hand under the wood and see if you find some ziti."

"No, but will it bite?"

"Bite? No, no! It's just a little round noodle!"

Brian, down below, rolled his eyes and sourly shook his head, then went about gingerly gathering wood in his arms, all the while peering at the hole into which the creature had skittered. His arms full, he walked past the jam shelf and the mushroom colony, and thumped up the steps to feed the fires.

It was daybreak; time to set off.

As the troll glared at the griddle, scratching the pan back and forth over the woodstove's burner, he apologized: "Oh, I'm sorry about the evil spirits last night. I didn't know that they were coming by, or I would have put up my protective amulets."

Gregory had entered the kitchen and slouched next to the troll with his hands slumped in his pockets. "What exactly happened last night?"

"What? When the evil spirits came?"

"Yes. When we found you in that fit."

The troll righted himself and quirked an eyebrow. "Pardon?"

"You were in a fit. Rolling around on the floor. It looked like you'd knocked the kitchen apart. Beastie Betty Crocker goes berserk."

"Hmm?"

"You were in the kitchen, after we fell asleep."

"Well, the demons came, all of them, and . . . I guess they left me like that. But I thought I remembered . . . well, hmm . . . odd, odd, odd! Couldn't you hear it? They were screaming and shouting? You must have heard! Zabbindathel was singing 'Last Train to Lyonesse.' Bad, bad, ve-he-he-he-ry bad!" he reported, shaking his head.

The boys uprighted the table and picked up the worst of the wreckage. They talked about where various things should be replaced. They threw away piles of smashed clay.

When Brian and Gregory were seated, Kalgrash slid their bowls to them across the table (the plates were mostly broken). Brian blinked nervously at the omelette, and even more so at the bowl of milk (the cups had been broken as well) that was deposited before him.

"Eat up!" said Gregory cheerfully, and plunged his fork vigorously into the steaming egg.

"Is something wrong?" asked Kalgrash through a mouth of pasty rabbit's pelt and omelette. "Can I get you something else?"

"Oh, no . . . no," protested Brian quickly.

Gregory smiled and exclaimed, "Well, good! Chow down! Soup's on!" and again launched into his food, chewing happily.

After a few minutes of this, it came to the surface that Brian was allergic both to milk and eggs, a revelation that Gregory treated with overwhelmed astonishment. Brian had ham and cider for breakfast.

"So where are you off to today? Going to try to get back into your uncle's house?"

"Are you kidding?" said Gregory. "Not if it had a drive-through window and to-go bags of free money."

"Do you think Prudence is safe?" Brian asked.

Gregory twisted his lips around, considering carefully. After a minute, he said, "I don't know. I hope so. What Uncle Max said makes sense. She would only be in danger as long as we were there. Otherwise, the Thussers don't have anything against her."

"So you want to keep going?" asked Brian.

Gregory thought for a minute. "Time's running out," he said. "Who knows where Jack Stimple is."

"We have the propeller now," said Brian. "We can head down the underground river. What do you think?"

Gregory nodded. "Sounds like a good idea to me."

After breakfast, they gathered their packs from the floor. They thanked their host, and he thanked them for saving him from his swoon. When they left him, he was rummaging around in a wooden chest to find a hammer and some nails.

They shook the troll's hand, and set off for their day's adventures. It was still raining lightly; however, the two suspected they would spend most of the day underground, anyway.

✳ ✳ ✳

After a long silence as they walked, Brian said thoughtfully, "It was strange, that fit he had last night."

"Ya. Evil spirits, I guess."

"Did you hear anything?"

"No. I slept like a log."

"Me, too. They sure weren't there when we woke up. They must have thrown him into that fit."

"Kalgrash is sort of hyperactive, anyway."

Brian glanced at Gregory. "He sort of reminds me of you, actually."

"Oh, thanks."

"No, no, I'm not kidding."

"What do you mean?"

"He bounces around and makes jokes."

"I don't bounce."

"You make jokes."

"I don't bounce. I can't believe you're saying I bounce."

Brian didn't say anything else. They kept on walking.

The two reached the folly at around nine o'clock. The stone was stained a dreary gray by water; the mosaics were now almost entirely obscured again by blackish mud. The boys heaved the plug out from the center of the floor and peered into the chilly chasm beneath.

"Great," said Gregory. "Nothing stopping us now." He fumbled along the wall for the lantern on the peg. "Nothing stopping us from going down right now." He held the lantern by its wire handle in his mouth and scrambled around with his packet of matches until one was lit. He muttered, through the wire, "Nothing stopping us from strolling right into whatever death pit waits for us." He touched the match to the lantern's wick, then held the lamp out in front of him. They descended into the cavity, carefully supporting themselves with the dank walls. "Nothing to stop us from being minced or ground up. Nothing to stop us from being drowned, burned, electrocuted, yanked apart, drilled . . ." The words became tinnier and tinnier, became lumps of echo without any sense. The day brightened as noon drew on. No sound came from below. A squirrel scampered across the floor of the pagoda and bounced his nose off the displaced stone plug a few times. Uninterested, she scurried off. Evening fell, and the wind picked up once again.

As darkness finally painted everything blue, an emaciated figure wrapped in a voluminous black cloak stalked up to the cavity, clicked his forked tongue, and swooped down upon the stone, slamming it back into place. Dissatisfied, he glared around the folly and finally set about scraping the leaves back into place again over the mosaics with his long, clawed foot. As he walked off, he muttered to himself in a grating, inhuman voice, "Untidy. Untidy . . ."

The wind tickled the leaves behind him.

✳   ✳   ✳

The boat sat where it had the other day. It knocked gently against the bank in response to some imperceptible current. The two approached it carefully. "Have you ever driven a motorboat before?" inquired Gregory.

"I've steered my uncle's sometimes," said Brian. "But I don't see any way to steer this boat. Unless we turn the whole motor by hand."

"We may have to." Gregory stepped onto the boat. It rocked briefly, until he stumbled into a sitting position on one of the seats. The flame in the lantern bobbed and flickered, sending reflections from the brass fittings whirling about the walls. "Well, get in."

Gregory rose to a stoop and helped Brian step in. "Now," said Brian. "We've got to put in the propeller."

"All right. You want to try that?"

Brian nodded. "Sure." Bending over so as not to rock the boat, he stepped to the back of the tiny craft and set down his pack to root around for the iron pinwheel. He drew it out of the bag and stood peering into the water, leaning with one arm on the rim of the boat. Gregory joined him.

"Here, do you want me to take your coat?" offered Gregory.

"Yeah." Brian stood and worked his way out of the tweed cloak, draping it over his friend's arm. He rolled up his shirt sleeves, then leaned forward again, got down on his knees, and dipped his hands into the frigid waters. "Shoot, it's cold." He carefully inserted the rod into the engine, screwing up his face in pain as he groped in the dark water. Gregory held the lantern closer.

"Have you got it?" he asked encouragingly.

Brian nodded and withdrew his arms. Shivering, he quickly daubed them dry with his coat. He pulled down his sleeves and fixed the cufflinks, then took his coat from Gregory. "It's in. It clicked. I guess we're ready to go, if this thing is really going to go anywhere."

Gregory said, "Before we go on, why don't we look at

the game board to see if it'll tell us any more, now that we found a solution to the propeller problem."

"Good idea," said Brian.

Gregory pulled out the ancient board, noticing that the strip of fabric that connected the two halves was becoming distinctly wobbly and frayed. He pried the boards open and inspected the game. "More spaces," he said. "We have two routes. Down the river that way is something called the Grinding Falls, where there's a box that says, 'Solve Riddle — Lose turns until Falls have been passed.' The other direction, we'll go through some cavern and across Lake Gwarnmore, then we go down the Taskwith Canal . . . and then we get to . . . oh, wonderful, yeah, the Steps of Doom, here, next to Snarth's Cavern, where we either solve a riddle or lose the game."

"Didn't we hear that name Snarth before?"

" 'Snarth'? Well, I mean, it's a common enough name — "

"No, no, no! The Club of Snarth, outside!"

"Hm, you're right," muttered Gregory. "That's great. That's really wonderful. . . . Well . . ." He scowled. "Which direction do we want to point the boat in? Snarth or falls?"

Brian reasoned through it. "Losing the game is worse than losing a turn. That's what we've seen. For example, Gelt the Winnower was more dangerous than Kalgrash. For Kalgrash, we were just stuck until we got an answer. With Gelt, he'd kill us." Brian considered, gripping the sides of the boat. He said, finally, "So I vote we go for Snarth."

Gregory looked startled. "What?"

"I think that the more difficult puzzles lead to the most direct route," said Brian. "The more we risk, the faster we go. And we've wasted a lot of time."

"Did someone take an idiot pill?"

"We're running out of time. We have, what, a couple of days, maybe?"

Gregory frowned and drummed his fingers on the seat. "You really want to?"

"How are we going to win, otherwise?" asked Brian.

"Okay," said Gregory. "Okay."

"This is the most direct route."

"Sure. To our butts in the fry-o-lator," Gregory muttered. "I know you're right, but I wish there was a route that involved complementary chocolates and a lawn chair."

"We're running out of time," said Brian. "Whoever those people are, they'll be in exile forever if we don't win."

"All right," said Gregory. "Okay. You're right. Let's detach these mooring things." They unclipped the chains from the shore and dropped them rattling into the hull of the boat. Slowly, the skiff drifted away from the rocky shore. "Turn the boat upstream," said Gregory, "if that's the way we're going." He waited, raised an eyebrow, and asked, "That's really the way you want to go?"

Brian thought long and hard about it. He steeled himself. Finally, he said, "It's strategy."

Gregory nodded, and they pushed off so the nose of the boat was pointing upstream. Gradually, they drifted backward.

"Well, Skipper, pull the lever," suggested Gregory.

Brian grasped hold of the lightning bolt lever and pulled it. The engine roared to life. The bronze elephant heads bobbed up and down, and the ivory glittered and spun. Behind the propeller, the water boiled. "I hope this is really what you want to do," yelled Gregory over the noise.

The boat steered itself. After puttering out into the middle of the stream, it headed against the current, under one of the arches. Gregory leaned forward and placed the lantern on the hook provided at the prow of the boat, and then sat back to survey the sights.

The boat chugged through a murky tunnel, the engine mercilessly loud in the confined space — the boys had to block their ears with their fingers. They drifted onward, turning as the tunnel turned, as if some invisible hand guided their journey.

The tunnel eventually widened out and, simultaneously, the noise of the engine grew softer, dimming to a subdued purr. The lantern creaked on its peg. The water dribbled past the prow of the boat. Through depths and deeper depths of darkness they drifted, past acres of stone and water.

They passed the front of a house that was carved into the sheer wall. Tall, slim windows were blocked by rusted iron gratings. The arched door was half-sunken in the river, opening out on steps that lay unevenly beneath the water. A mooring column rose from the river. "Like Venice," whispered Gregory, and Brian nodded.

The river widened into a vast lake — Lake Gwarnmore — a lake so wide and dark that even when Gregory rose and held up the lantern, squinting to see the shore, they could discern nothing but darkness. Gregory sighed, hung up the lantern, and sat again.

At one point, they thought they perceived other boats on the lake. They seemed to hear the trickling of water from oars and the splash of rowing. They both scrambled to their feet and stared around, straining to hear through the rumble of the motor. They thought they saw, across the glossy water, the flash of a wet surface, the glitter of metal.

Brian grabbed the lever and flung it upward. The motor chugged spasmodically and halted. They sat for a while, frozen and aching, until finally the silence in the cavern became even more worrisome than the noise had been. Brian pulled the lever, and they continued on their way.

It seemed to take ages to cross the lake. Although Brian still gazed around him at the chilly shadows, Gregory gave up and inspected the herringbone pattern of his knickerbockers.

Finally, they glimpsed a new wall ahead of them, this time featureless except for a towering, ornately carved archway, vines tangled with pointy-eared cherubs and sprigs of laurel. "Wow," exclaimed Gregory quietly. The skiff passed through the mammoth arch, into a narrower passage. Heavy lanterns — huge, grimy globes on complex iron frameworks — projected from the walls. They passed windows and doors.

After a while, the boat puttered to the bank and nuzzled the shore at the foot of a wide stone staircase. Next to it there were two mooring clips like those at the Dark Marina. Cautiously, the two boys rose, and each pulled out a chain, running the links between their fingers as they stretched them to the shore. They clipped the boat into place, then Brian shut off the engine.

Their ears whined and rang in the sudden silence.

"Well," said Gregory. "Here we are."

Brian nodded.

"So do we go find out what Snarth is?" asked Gregory.

"Sure," said Brian.

Gregory nodded and unhooked the lantern from the front of the boat. He muttered, "And you're the one who's supposed to be the coward."

"I'm scared," Brian admitted.

"Good," said Gregory. " 'Cause so am I."

They peered around suspiciously, and began climbing the Steps of Doom. The soles of their shoes scratched dryly over the stone. The shadows wavered. At the top of the stairs, a large archway awaited them, a little wooden doorway in the side. Standing on the top step, Gregory flung his arm forward, holding the lantern bravely into the next cavern. The lantern creaked on its wire and swung slowly back and forth.

The flame illuminated dark, uneven grottos, thin columns of natural stone, uneven floors and, on the other side of the cavern, another natural archway. The two boys blinked, their hearts racing. Brian stepped forward and squinted. His hand rose nervously to the strap of his knapsack, where it hung on his shoulder. No sound stirred the air.

"Well?" said Gregory.

Brian shrugged, still looking into the cavern. They ran their eyes quickly over the surfaces of mottled stone again. Then they heard the snore — it sounded at first like stone ponderously scraping stone. There was a hiss of escaping breath. Then silence again. The two stood perfectly still. A muscle in Gregory's leg was twitching. Another snore growled through the chamber, then the hiss, then the silence.

The two looked at each other, their eyes wide. Brian licked his lips. He remembered Jack Stimple's words — nothing protected the two of them, nothing here cared whether they lived or died.

Gregory nodded, a prompt for them to creep forward. He stepped quietly across the threshold into the cavern. Brian followed. The light-haired boy was as silent as a cat as he crossed the vast floor. His companion was as quiet as he could manage. Then they saw Snarth.

He was prone against a boulder. He was maybe twenty feet tall, a huge and warty ogre, eyeless, his thick nose with two huge nostrils dripping over a mouth with two dirty yellow tusks. His massive limbs, draped with muscle and fat, were curled uncomfortably on his belly. He wore a skirt of furs.

The two were very careful. They did not make a sound.

But still, the nostrils began to twitch. The golden hairs in them began delicately to wave. Then the massive head started to rock.

And the beast sat up.

Shaking its head and grumbling, "Mmm, mm, hm . . . ,"

the giant crawled to his feet wearily. He sniffed at the air, his hands outspread. The two boys froze with fear. Snarth sighed, then grimaced. He rotated his shoulders a few times, and wriggled both of his huge legs in turn.

Then, with an insane yowl, he leaped across the chamber and tromped on the spot where the boys had been; he stomped vigorously so as to ensure that any life there had been extinguished.

SEVENTEEN

The two boys had thrown themselves through the next archway and down a vast set of stairs as the ogre prepared for his leap. They heard him stomping, they heard his mindless yowling, they could hear his pause and his mucoid sniffing.

As they reached the bottom of the stairs, the flame picked out details of things around them — the side of a house with a steep, steep roof, a house encrusted with some kind of convoluted carving.

Gregory and Brian breathlessly charged down a shoddily cobbled street. Snarth bellowed behind them as he leaped to the foot of the stairs.

"House!" screamed Gregory, and he pulled off to the left, grabbing at Brian's sleeve as he passed him. The two scurried through the door and through the empty stone chambers within. They stood shivering in a back room that had no windows, the rumble of Snarth's angry

breath echoing in to them as he stooped before the minute doorway.

"This is great," whispered Gregory. "Superb choice." And then, as if swearing, he said over and over again, "Thank you, thank you, thank you."

Brian said, "Look. There must be other windows we can crawl out of. On another side of the house."

Gregory nodded and stepped quickly through to another room, this one bare like the last. They went up a flight of stairs.

In the upstairs rooms, windows looked from gables and walls out to the back of the house — but they were thirty feet off the ground. Gregory leaned out of the casement and twisted around to look upward. He couldn't see anything above them. The light from the lantern illuminated only the leering gargoyles that perched on every corner, that slithered over every lintel, that squatted on every gable of the house opposite.

Gregory crept to the front window. Below, he could see Snarth standing, his arms crossed impatiently, snorting suspiciously at the air. They could hear his breath, the whine of air through cavernous sinuses and stalagmites of snot.

They waited. The ogre hunkered down and stuck his nose through the door. He stood again, scratching his chin. He paced a few steps to the left, then changed his mind, and paced a few steps to the right.

And then, quick as lightning, he grabbed on to windows and began climbing. He heaved himself upward.

The boys stumbled back; they ran for the stairs. The ogre charged up and started fumbling his blunt fingers around in the room. They threw themselves downward, slamming into walls.

Out the front door. They ran for a side street. Snarth had his arm stuck in the window. He teetered there. Smelled them. Started to yank his arm out.

They were running through an alley. Found it led right back to Snarth's cavern. He was thumping down the street toward them.

"There was a door on the other side of the cavern! There was a little door!" Brian screamed.

They crossed the floor of Snarth's den. Brian was red-faced; he had fallen behind. Gregory had always been better at running. He had won the school marathon. He tugged at Brian. Brian was slow.

Snarth had reached the entrance of the cavern. He leaped.

They were crawling, stooping, and running, tripping . . . Gregory had found the little wooden door in the wall. *"Brian!"* he shouted. Brian was there at his side — Brian banged his nose on the edge of the door, his glasses fell — the ogre was right behind them — Brian gasped — but his glasses landed on his crumpled sleeve, and he grabbed them, and went around the door, and felt Gregory pull up on his collar — and he ran forward — and tripped over a stair — and the blunt fingers came scuttling up toward him — and he scrambled on hands and knees upward.

It was a spiral flight of stairs. The hairy arm shot around the bend. Brian and Gregory could hear the soft shuffling of his fingers behind them. They fell over each other, and their packs rattled wildly.

But they were far enough up that he couldn't reach them.

They crawled on up for ages, gasping for breath, until they heard the angry cries of the ogre far below them. Then Gregory rose and unslung his pack. Brian leaned against the wall, feeling slick sweat prickle in all of his pores, feeling his body shudder at each stampeding heartbeat.

"Okay," said Gregory, "so it wasn't a great idea to try to get past Snarth."

Brian didn't respond.

"What? Are you mad at me?" said Gregory. "You're mad at something."

Brian just said, "We need to figure out how to get around him."

Gregory nodded, his light hair hanging limply over his eyes, darker than usual with sweat.

He made no cracks.

They kept on ascending the staircase.

✳ ✳ ✳

They emerged from a splintered door in an old foundation a few hours later. The foundation, lined with bulging stones, had been filled with spiky bushes and ferns in the summer. The ferns had withered, and the bushes were reduced to crackling skeletons, easy to push aside with a well-placed foot.

The two pulled themselves out of the pit and peered around them in the twilight to get their bearings. They were on the side of the mountain; the ground was steeply pitched. Tall pines crowded thickly around them on the slope, turning dark blue in the falling darkness. A late bat swung above their heads and disappeared into the top of the pines.

Gregory suggested, "We should probably make a campfire and settle down for the night. There's no way we'll find our way back to Uncle Max's or Kalgrash's in the dark. And we don't know what's waiting for us back at Uncle Max's, anyway."

"Okay," said Brian. "Maybe we should move away from the door to the caverns, just in case someone else uses it." He considered for a moment, staring blankly at his shoe. "We can scuff the pine needles to make sure we can find our way back in the morning. If we want to."

"Yeah, I'm not particularly looking forward to a walk down all those stairs and another battle with Snarth, myself."

"Yeah," said Brian unhappily.

They set off, Brian dragging his foot determinedly to make a dark trail in the dirt. The woods were silent, save for a bit of wind that occasionally rattled branches and set pine needles rustling. Gregory shivered with the cold.

After a while, they came to another clearing. Night had definitely fallen. Many stars were out, although to one side a great bank of softly moonlit clouds obscured them. The two gathered sticks and made a fire; they had learned how during their disastrous stint as Cub Scouts. Most of the time had been spent spelling out the Pledge of Allegiance with alphabet noodles.

The fire going, they heated up some of the food that the servants had packed in their rucksacks. Then they spread out their bedrolls on either side of the flames, crawled in clumsily without taking off their overcoats (it was very chilly), and lay staring up at the sky.

Gregory looked at his friend across the flames. Then he said, "Hey. We're risking our lives together." He held up his fist. "This is what friends are for. Thank you." When Brian didn't say anything, he continued. "At least we know that normal is out of the question for us now. Suits and nine to five. Now we know we'll have to really do something with our lives. You can go on to become a famous journalist. I'll be the world's first skateboarding bishop."

Finally, Brian smiled. He said softly, "I guess once you've had breakfast with a troll, there's no going back."

Gregory nodded. He settled down in his bedroll. "Good night," he said, and Brian answered, "Good night."

They both curled up in their blankets, crooking their hands beneath their faces. Whenever a root or a stone became intolerable, they would rustle around until they had eased the ache. The fire dimmed. Once, Brian woke up to see a raccoon staring at the fire, but he faded back to sleep.

Above them, the stars revolved. For a time, they were not the stars of Earth. A second moon rose above the mountain. But in the deepest part of the night it faded and, by dawn, the sky was back to normal.

EIGHTEEN

The two were walking on a path around the mountainside.

"I'm not going back down there," said Gregory.

"There must be a way past him, though," figured Brian. "We just have to think how."

"Sure."

"Every time we've come up against one of those 'Solve the Riddle' things, we've needed one specific thing to solve the puzzle — like the weathervane and the propeller. Something we knew about that we had to connect with the puzzle."

"Say, do you think that soup tureen at Uncle Max's is a panzer tank in disguise?"

In the light of day, they could see that a well-worn path rambled away in either direction from the old cellar. They randomly chose a branch and began marching resolutely down it. Surrounded by the dark fir trees, the boys were protected from much of the frigid wind that muscled its way between the swaying treetops.

They had traveled for about an hour, recognizing nothing, getting nowhere, high up on the mountain when, in the midst of a gully edged by boulders, the path ended abruptly at a sign reading TURN BACK. DO NOT ENTER.

"This is a little shabby," Gregory complained. "You'd think that with hundreds of miles of forest, they could at least manage to hide things better than this."

Brian peered past the boulders and into the woods. "Do you want to leave the path?"

"Sure."

"But what happens if we're found out?"

"I dunno. We get mangled."

The boy strode off toward the forest, stepping up onto the rocks. Brian followed him.

Forging their path was difficult: Branches scraped them, hidden rocks tripped them (Brian especially), and dirt gave way beneath their shoes.

Eventually they broke out of the wood. Large boulders lay about, lime-green with lichen, surrounded by thick blueberry bushes. Gregory scrambled up onto one of the boulders and turned around to survey the land above the trees. "Brian, come look!" Brian stepped up to his side.

Above the pines, they could see the land that lay around the mountain far below.

Hills rose and fell, the trees painted in impossible colors; in the distance, great blue mountains towered from the patchwork earth. Small dips where creeks ran, a few browning pastures, an occasional black roof or white steeple — these were the only features that broke the continuous expanse of glowing forest.

They could see the places they had wandered in the course of the week, laid out almost as clearly as on the gameboard. The mansion, with its lawns around it, smoke curling from its chimney; the Ceremonial Mound, rising dark, far, far below; the Crooked Steeple and the ruined Grendle house; the woods; the bridge; and the River of Time and Shadow, which ran under a distant road, past Gerenford Green, joining other rivers until, in the blue distance, it flowed through mill towns and suburbs and under highways and led, eventually, to the distant city the boys called home, and from there, into the sea.

They stood there several minutes, watching the distant trees sway in the breeze.

The clouds drifted across the crisp sky.

They felt the wind all around them.

✳　✳　✳

An hour later, they were far above the tree-line. The climbing was getting harder. There were wide granite faces all around them.

That is when they came upon a door in the stone.

On the door, there was a brass sign that read WEE SNIGGLEPING.

"Eh," said Gregory. "Isn't that cute."

Brian stepped up to the door and knocked.

There was a pause of a few seconds before the latch handle snapped up and the door opened. A little man stood there, shorter than either of them — a bald little man, dressed in a red vest and skewed round glasses. His ears were distinctly pointed. He had on a hat made of owl feathers, dried swamp flowers, and pipe cleaners.

"Yes, hello," he said, looking impatiently from one boy to the other.

Brian ventured, "Um, we were out walking and we, we got a little lost, and thought you might help us find the way."

"Hmm! The 'way' to what? A refreshment stand? You're on a mountaintop. Top of a mountain. Hmm? Savvy?"

Gregory cleared his throat. The man glanced up at the boy, one elfin eyebrow cocked suspiciously. Gregory said, "You're Sniggleping, then?"

"Yes."

"An elf."

"Close enough."

Gregory simply nodded. "Yup," he said.

There was an awkward silence for everybody. Gregory tried to fill it by wearily clapping his hands together.

Sniggleping inquired, "You're not playing the Game, are you?"

"Yes," said Brian.

"You are. I see. You're playing." The elf-man rapped his knuckles angrily against the door frame. He turned and walked back into his house. "Come in," he said. "You're out of bounds. The Thusser will be having an absolute fit." The door was still open. Brian followed him, with Gregory tailing close behind, hands jammed in his pockets, head bowed down so his light hair swung before his eyes.

Sniggleping's peculiar apartment was one room on

two levels, with a small flight of stairs leading to the loft. The place was a shambles, crammed with great cogwheels and boxes of bolts, wrenches and hammers and hack-saws, huge leather portfolios of diagrams, half-constructed engines of brass and ivory, welding tools wired to dismantled lightning rods, crystal balls of various sizes, obsidian pentagrams and, over the mantel, some sort of stuffed beast that either had one leg too many or one leg too few, depending on how you counted them. The two stood uncomfortably while the wizened elf gabbled nonsense syllables into the horn of an Edwardian telephone.

Brian glanced at one of the plans that lay on the table. Snarth the ogre was drawn upon it, colored in full, gruesome detail, with all the warts marked. Arrows jabbed at particular features on the monstrous body, labeled in the illegible runic language. A windup key was drawn protruding from his back.

Sniggleping slammed down the phone and turned to them. "Right. That's that."

"We should probably go," said Brian. "We're sorry for getting off the path."

"Stay here," said Sniggleping. "Talk."

"No," said Brian. "We should — "

"Talk."

"Okay," said Gregory. He moved over to examine the diagram of Snarth more closely. "What are these diagrams for?"

"By 'talk,' I meant about something else, like boating or sleet."

"These look like Snarth," said Gregory.

"All right, get away from those!"

"What are they?"

"Nothing."

Gregory said, "Did you build the ogre?"

"Yes. Yes. So?"

"So it's a machine?"

"Would you stop it with the questions?" shouted Sniggleping. "Yes. Nothing you'd understand. Yes." He began to mutter, pacing back and forth, his hands forced into gnarled fists, his wrists flexing this way and that. Gregory and Brian continued to stare at him. He looked up after a moment and shouted fiercely, "Don't look at me like I've just sat on your pet goldfish! So the ogre's a fake, all right? Do you know how hard it is to find an ogre these days? No — no! Not just hard! Impossible. *Im! Poss! Ib! Ul!*"

Brian assured him, "We didn't mean to — "

"Do you know how long it took me to make that ogre? Do you know the technologies necessary? Do you know the scaffolding that has to be assembled every time we want to wind the thing up? Does that sound like fun? No! Does it sound easy? No! No! No!"

He stormed over to a table, threw around some sprawling blueprints, and finally flung a few off the balcony at the boys. *"And look at these!"*

The papers drifted to the ground, sliding against one another as they came to rest. Brian and Gregory inspected them. Gregory said, "Burk and Daffodil. Burk. Whoa."

"Yes, yes, *YES!* They wanted servants down at the mansion. But *no,* they couldn't be silent servants, they had to *talk*! And *no,* they didn't just have to *talk,* they had to have a whole *history.* Personalities! *Do you know how long that took?* Weeks of nailing and wiring and summoning!"

He wrinkled his lips and kicked a gremlin-formed banister. After a minute, he looked up again. "Oh, you don't understand, do you? It's the little things that make a Game good."

Brian protested, "We've appreciated it a lot."

Gregory said, "Yeah, when you're being killed by something cool, you really appreciate the hard time and effort someone —"

Brian said, "We didn't mean to upset you or make it seem —"

"*Why? Who am I? Just an 'elf'!* Living under a *rock*! Oh, wait! I'm supposed to live in a *tree,* right? And *HAND-MAKE DOUBLE-FUDGE COOKIES! 'Oh, what wonderful wafers! What great wafers you have, elfy!' IS THAT WHAT YOU'RE THINKING? HUH? HUH? THAT'S IT, NO? NO?*" He bellowed, then kicked a chair full of blueprints so hard that they flew up into the air and slid in a heavy mass across the floor.

Gregory looked at Brian.

Brian seemed to have suddenly thought of something awful. He had frozen. He didn't look well.

Sniggleping collapsed back into a cluttered chair, his knuckly hands wrapped around his face. He slouched in the seat as blueprints of a three-headed pterodactyl slid out from underneath his rear.

Brian said carefully, "What other . . . what other creatures have you made that have been difficult?"

Sniggleping glared out from between his fingers. "Oh, no. No, no, no. You're going to have to figure the Game out for yourself. No, no, no, no, no. Sniggleping's too clever by half. Hah. No, it's not all me, kiddies. Some of it was here long before me. Some of it was imported from distant places. Some of it stumbles in from other worlds when the stars lock up." He dropped his hands from his face and stared at a chandelier that lit the place, draped with drying bow ties. "And to do it all with amateurs," he said wearily. "I used to work on the city, when the Emperor Taskwith was here. When the People of Norumbega were here. Before they all fled. And now?"

Brian asked quietly, "The troll," he said. "Did you make Kalgrash?"

"He's one of mine," said Sniggleping. "Miserable job. Never really worked out all the kinks. He gets seizures whenever the Ceremonial Mound is active. Hallucinations. It runs complete haywire with his brain. Oh," he said, frowning at the boys, "I guess I should stick to what I'm good at, hmm? Little elfy? Stick to what he's good at? *Huh? TOWN HOUSE CRACKERS —*" He yelled, banging his fist, *"THAT RIGHT? MAKING! YOUR! TOWN! HOUSE! CRACKERS?!?"*

The latch rattled. The door swung open, creaking slightly on its hinges. A dark cape blocked most of the sunlight from outside. The creature stepped in, ducking to avoid hitting its head.

"Thank God you got here," said Sniggleping. "They're driving me loopy." To the boys he said, "Speculant."

The Speculant was about eight feet tall, and was far bonier beneath his heavy black cape than any human could ever have been — even if their legs, like his, bent backward at the knees. He wore a black hat with an exceedingly wide brim over a face that consisted of little but an impossibly long, spiky nose, not unlike Kalgrash's — almost, in his case, a beak. His alien skin was the kaleidoscope browns of a moth's wings. Spiny fingers like jointed twigs clutched at the cape, flexing and pulling restlessly.

"Don't stay and talk," said Sniggleping. "Take them away. How you let this happen, I don't know."

The Speculant spoke. His voice was deep and grainy, and sounded as if it were echoing in a tunnel. "The darkness fell on the Flower That Speaks No Riddles, and — "

"Oh, don't give me that."

"Come," ordered the phantom-like figure, sweeping his gaunt arms in a wide gesture. "The Boundaries that are set in fire have cried with their siren voices, for you stepped through the Bounding Stones into the Unwritten Places, where no hand has scrawled with Quill Supernal." And then he repeated, "Come with me."

The boys moved slowly toward the door, the towering Speculant falling in behind them, his fingers clutched together in front of his chest.

"Uh, good-bye," said Brian.

Sniggleping answered, "Just shut the door."

So they did.

They stood outside, once more in the glaring daylight and the chilly breeze.

"Follow," beckoned the Speculant, and he glided off into the wood.

The two moved to keep up with him. The Speculant loped up rock faces, drifted down pathways, and floated between the trees, occasionally turning silently to wait for them.

Gregory watched Brian walk along ahead of him. Brian seemed preoccupied. He was frowning slightly, and did not speak.

Finally, they reached the remains of a ruined square tower that jutted out of the boulders and dreary grasses of the mountainside. "It stands from the epoch when these mountains," said the Speculant, "were coated in metal, when from the Gulf Unknown the Enemy issued." He ducked inside, and the two friends followed him.

The interior of the tower was a void, most of the floors evidently having collapsed centuries before. They walked down an old staircase into the shadows of a deep basement. There were occasionally passages branching off to the sides. When Gregory asked where these went, the Speculant just replied, "The corridor of Truth lies closed; the darkness of the Unspoken Void yawns closer."

"Huh?" said Gregory. He tried to catch Brian's eye, but Brian wasn't listening. Brian looked miserable.

"The Day approaches when the Vast One shall be greater than He Who Found the Key. Then shall we all be left upon the Plain That Has No Name."

Gregory coaxed, "Oh, come on . . . they could give the plain a name! Any old thing would do!"

"When the Time of Naming arrives, then shall the unnamed and unnameable be called by its True Name."

"I'll bet it has a name, and you just can't remember it, you sly devil."

The Speculant swiveled around, his cape settling around him slowly. He grated, "The Unnameable has no Name. Truth cannot be concealed behind Fiction. The Casket of Deliverance has found the Pearl of Wisdom lacking, and the Bone of No Sight shall, in the latter — "

"Okay," said Gregory. "You win."

The Speculant waited.

"Really," said Gregory. "Ten nothing. Your game." He nodded. "More walk, less talk."

The Speculant nodded triumphant, turned, and walked on.

They came to a dimly lit chamber, in which there were broken arches and columns all around them. The Speculant continued out into the center of the floor, his feet whispering on the dry dust. Gregory and Brian followed him.

When they reached him, standing by his side amidst the fallen columns and echoes, he swept up his arms and chanted in his gravelly voice. The words fluttered through the chamber, echoing and re-echoing, until finally they faded.

Silence closed back in around them, save that they heard, only faintly, an odd, sandy shuffling in the unlit recesses and colonnades. "This way," beckoned the

Speculant, and he drifted away across the floor. He led them to a small archway, beneath which they ducked, and up a ladder. He halted at the top.

With a heave, he reached above him and shoved a heavy iron disk to the side. Light streamed in from above. He climbed the last few rungs. They followed. Gregory, at the top of the ladder, looked back down toward Brian. He was concerned. Brian was moving slowly. It looked like something was weighing on him. They went up the ladder.

They found themselves blinking and squinting in the bright sunlight, closely surrounded by an entangled knot of hemlocks. They were in a small clearing at the top of a thickly wooded knoll. A ring of tall stones was there. Nearby was a tent, with Jack Stimple's hat hanging on the tent pole. When they looked at their feet, they saw that there was no sign of the manhole cover that the Speculant had thrown aside. "Do not look for the passage. It would not take you back where we came from. Now follow me."

The figure darted into the underbrush and followed a hectic, zigzag course down the steep side of the knoll. The two tripped and climbed after him, finally emerging from the trees.

They discovered, finally, where they were. They had come out on top of the Ceremonial Mound. Now they were back by the burnt-out snowmobile, in the midst of the Tangled Knolls.

"Do you see where you are?" said the Speculant.

"Yes," said Brian.

"Very good. The Game must now continue. Do not

venture off the paths. You are but Pawns. You can be Taken. Go."

"What do you mean, 'Taken'?" asked Gregory.

"Snatched up in moment," said the Speculant. "By a gaunt hand."

Gregory smiled. "Great. Well, it's been nice talking to you. Thank you very much."

Brian suddenly exclaimed, "Wait! We're going to need the boat to get back into the cavern! It's at the wrong end of its route!"

The Speculant nodded his proboscis. "Yes. Go." He pointed forcibly toward one of the many paths that led away from the Ceremonial Mound.

Gregory and Brian left him standing there. They walked away, into the forest.

He turned and climbed back into the hemlocks of the Mound.

NINETEEN

I don't know what all that was about," said Gregory.

Brian didn't answer.

Gregory continued, "I mean, beyond the obvious. The Plain That Has No Name. The Plateau That Cannot Be Uttered. The Butte We Just Don't Talk About."

"Yeah," said Brian.

"What's the matter?" asked Gregory.

"Gregory . . . ," said Brian. He didn't continue.

"Come on. We need to think about how to get past the ogre."

Brian nodded. After a minute, though, he said, "I'm worried about Kalgrash."

Gregory said, "You think he's a machine."

Brian frowned. "And I think he doesn't know it."

Gregory clamped his hands under his arms. He bit his lip. "Hey," he said, his face brightening. "I got it. I think I've got it!"

"What?"

"The next object we have to use. To get past the ogre. I figured it out."

Brian rubbed his scalp. He said, "I wasn't even thinking about that."

Gregory, caught up in his own enthusiasm, began kicking a stick back and forth across the clearing. He chased it. "Aren't you going to ask?" he said.

Brian sighed. "Go ahead."

"Snarth has no eyes. He found us with his sense of smell." Gregory kept playing soccer with his stick. "What we have to do is get rid of our smell."

"Uh-huh," said Brian. His eyes were on the ground.

"The perfume! The scentless de-scentifying perfume! We have to put on the scentless perfume from the basement."

Brian nodded.

Gregory passed the stick to Brian. The stick hit Brian's leg and stopped. Gregory said, "Aren't you proud of me?"

"Sure," said Brian, like he wasn't.

"What's wrong?"

Brian shrugged.

"The house," said Gregory, slowing down. "This means we're going to have to go back to the house. I don't even want to know what's going on in there by now. This is going to be terrifying. A real adventure."

"Your Uncle Max said Prudence would be safe."

"Yeah," said Gregory, "but are *we*?" He slapped Brian on the arm. "Let's go," he went on. "We'll talk about how we're going to get in on the way."

Gregory set off, and Brian followed him.

"Can we just not talk for a minute?" said Brian.

"We need to have a strategy."

"There are other things we need to talk about."

"Look," said Gregory, "we'll see Kalgrash on the way, okay?"

Brian nodded. Gregory was walking ahead of him, so he didn't see.

They found their way through the Tangled Knolls and wandered through the woods. The leaves were somber — dark browny violets and lusterless browns. As they crossed the Golden Field toward the Troll Bridge, they heard Kalgrash singing to himself in a high, whistling voice. The words were not in English.

He was fishing off the bridge, humming and singing some weird waltz. He reeled in his line and swung the rod over his head in a flourish. He cast far off down the river.

He saw the boys walking toward him down the bank.

"Howdy!" he crowed. "How did things go? Solve it all yet?"

Gregory and Brian waved feebly and walked solemnly across the bridge toward him. Their caps were missing, their overcoats bore dark, dirty stains, their scarves sprouted numerous pulls, and their blankets hung slightly out of their bulging backpacks.

"Hey, hey, hey! What's the matter?"

"Um, hi," said Brian.

Gregory walked forward and went behind the troll. Kalgrash protested, "Hey, what's going on?"

"Just stand still for a second," Gregory ordered quietly. He ran his hand along the troll's slick back. "I'm looking for something."

"Gregory . . . ," warned Brian.

"What's wrong? Hey, are you taping something back there? 'Kick me' or something?"

Gregory said, "Here. Feel this."

The troll bent his elbow backward and poked with his spindly finger at the spot where Gregory had tapped. "Oh. Back acne again. It used to happen all the time," he explained nervously.

Gregory said, "See, Kalgrash . . ."

Brian interrupted him. "Gregory," he said. "I don't know . . ."

"What?" said Kalgrash. "Tell me."

Gregory explained, "We've just been up to the top of the mountain. We found some elf or something . . . someone named Sniggleping. He makes magical mechanical creatures and people. He . . . told us about them. He said that they have holes in their backs, where you have to stick a key to wind them up."

"What do you mean? Oh, hey . . . yeah, sure, funny."

Gregory and Brian looked at each other. "No," said Brian. "We're not kidding."

"Oh, come on. You're kidding."

Brian and Gregory just were silent. Kalgrash looked from one to the other. Kalgrash said, "You're trying to convince me I'm some machine?"

Brian said gently, "I'm . . . afraid so. The elf talked about fits that you might go through when there's magical activity at the Ceremonial Mound. The fits . . . they sound like what happened the other night. When you were visited by those 'evil spirits.'"

"But, I *see* them! Wabimalech the Destroyer, and Flaëlphagor the Drooling One. They come to my house! They pull things off the walls! You saw the mess they made. . . ."

Brian shook his head. "We saw you lying on the floor, in some kind of a coma. If you hadn't told us it was evil spirits, we would have thought that you'd just had a fit and broken everything up. There was really no sign that anyone else had been there. We just assumed it."

"I've *seen* them!" the troll protested. "More often than I've seen you! That's what they do — they spend their nights carousing, breaking things up, and their days watching television and eating Count Chocula out of the box."

Gregory turned away, frowning, and leaned his palms on the railing of the bridge.

Kalgrash said, "Hey, I bet you guys are kidding me, huh? A little joke, and you're about to yell surprise or something? I mean, it's not my birthday or anything, is it?"

"Kalgrash," Brian interjected miserably, bowing his head.

"What?" said the troll. "What?!?"

Brian asked quietly, "Why did you follow the Speculant's commands? What makes you want to stop people on the bridge and tell them the riddle?"

"Well, I just . . . I feel it. It's just who I am. It's what makes sense. What do you mean?"

"I think . . . ," said Brian, ". . . I think that maybe it's what you were made to do . . . I don't mean that in a way like . . ." But he couldn't think of anything else to say, and they all fell silent.

Hesitantly, the troll reached back and felt the spot on his back again. It was unmistakable — although invisible, there was a small metal ring there, where one could insert a key. Suddenly, the troll protested, "But I have all my memories! I remember everything! Well, not everything, but some things. I just can't be a machine."

"It . . . it doesn't matter, Kalgrash," Brian soothed awkwardly.

"I'm not a machine! I'm not! I'm not! I'm not!" shouted the troll. His shout turned to a whimper. "I'm not." He paused, staring down between the slats of the railing to where slick boulders glistened beneath the frigid river water. "My memories . . . what about them?"

"Programmed," said Gregory from the railing.

Brian glared at Gregory, and quickly supplied, "The elf, he said he'd made complete memories for the servants up at the house. He . . ."

"It can't be. What if I'm . . . but I . . ." The troll leaned his fishing rod against the railing and sat down, his legs dangling over the edge. "Not real. None of it. Made for your Game. Hah. Clockwork and gears." He reached up slowly and put his hand to where his heart beat. "Clockwork and gears. Pistons." Brian sat next to him. The troll didn't look up, but merely said, "Available while supplies last. Limited warrantee." Angrily, he added, "It's not true. It's not!"

Brian stared guiltily at the water. He urged, without much conviction, "We're . . . we're all machines, really, Kalgrash. That's the thing. Our heart's just a machine, too — a biological machine. No magic whatsoever. Our brain — it's just electrical signals. See, it's not that different. I mean, you at least have magic worked into your system. We don't. We're just plain matter."

"Yeah . . . yeah. Thank you," said the troll, subdued, nodding. He stood up. "Excuse me," he said quietly. "I'm . . . I'm going for a little walk. Go in and get yourselves something to eat or something and I'll . . . I'll be back in a few minutes."

"We'll — why don't we come back here in a couple of hours?" said Brian. "We have to go to the house to get something to solve a riddle. On the way back, we'll stop here and see . . . how you're . . . doing."

"If you want to," said the troll. "If." He nodded. He slowly walked to the end of the bridge and tromped off along the shore.

Gregory turned and looked after him, hands in pockets, then moved to stand next to Brian. Brian moved the other way. He didn't want to watch the troll. He could tell the troll didn't want to be watched.

"Let's keep walking," said Brian.

They headed toward the mansion.

Brian was miserable. "We shouldn't have told him," he said.

"Yeah," said Gregory. "We should have let it drop."

"Why did you tell him in the first place?"

Gregory kicked his way through the leaves. Neither of them spoke.

They kept walking toward the house.

* * *

The troll wandered down along the river, picking his way over boulders and browning moss, leaping over rivulets. Dead leaves were flying downstream, dipping and twirling as they bounced through pools and over currents.

Kalgrash thought about what he should do. He could race up the mountain, ax in his hand, and find the elf who had been so callous as to create him just for a Game. He knew that would be a troll's solution. Most people like to take apart their problems, look at them in smaller, more manageable pieces. Trolls, he mused, simply take this to the extreme. Trolls get a certain satisfaction out of seeing their enemies made insignificant and ridiculous — harmless pieces, spread over a room. *No*, he decided, *not that*. He was not a troll, after all. He was a bad imitation.

A sour sickness came over him at the thought of his pathetic jokes, his stupid innocence — he had been made to be silly, been made imperfect. Every thought was a whir of gears; even the thought that every thought was a whir of gears was just a whir of gears. He could break down, like the stove or plumbing, frizzled by lightning or local spell-casting interference. He watched his knees work as he walked, his arms shift to balance him, and thought, *What spindly, ridiculous little limbs. What a stupid shape.*

The last of the geese were flying overhead, honking in V-formation.

Kalgrash walked along on a path he had made over the last few years that rambled beside the moss-covered slabs surrounding the river. He broke out of the forest into a field where, sometimes, there were cows kept by a farm nearby. The cows weren't there.

Kalgrash crossed the field, the dead yellow grasses thrashing around his legs. Under a shadowy stand of maples, there was a plot marked out with an old black iron fence. As Kalgrash forced open the rusty gate, he plucked off the leaves that were impaled on the spikes of the fence.

He stood inside the plot, looking from stone to leaf-clogged stone. His eyes passed from Elijah Newcastle to Betty Newcastle without registering the names. He walked between the slate markers to two wooden crosses jammed into the ground at lopsided angles. His father and mother. What, he wondered, would he find if he dug down? Didn't he remember digging them, one by one, on wintry days?

All I have is memories, he mused. But if his parents had been real — if bodies had really been lying there inert in those graves, beneath those crosses — if there had been a mother who wore a flowered apron and spoke softly with a Scandinavian accent, a father who wore cologne and carved oak grizzlies for tourists with his axe — even if these things he remembered were true — then still, all he would have would be memories. They were good memories.

The flowers were withering on his fake mother's grave. He would have to bring her some more. They would curl and brown above the empty earth where she didn't lie.

The geese were passing over. Great storm clouds were gathering in the south — he could feel them — and they would sweep north, leaving winter wherever they passed.

TWENTY

The last time they had seen the house, it had been night, and it had been swarming with half-seen beasts. Now it stood tall and quiet in the cold autumn air, the sun throwing stripes across the roofs from the many chimneys.

The boys faced it across the lawns. Somehow, they had to get in.

"Think the best way is through the kitchen?" Gregory asked.

Brian shrugged. He didn't seem very energetic.

Gregory said, "The perfume is in the basement, which is off the kitchen."

'What about the Lurker?"

"Hmm?"

"The Basement Lurker," said Brian. "Uncle Max said that if the light went out, the Basement Lurker would seize us."

"That," said Gregory, wagging his finger, "that's a

bridge we'll cross when we come to it." He was looking nervously up toward the house.

"We should wait until tonight," said Brian. "When everyone's asleep."

"We don't have time," said Gregory. "Who knows where Jack Stimple is by now? We only have maybe a day left. We can't wait. And plus, I don't think anyone's sleeping in there much anymore."

"What do you mean?" said Brian.

"Let's go for the kitchen door," said Gregory.

They ran forward, crouching low. There were fewer windows in the back of the house; the rooms that looked out over the gardens were the servants' quarters, the kitchen, the nursery, and a bathroom. They saw no motion inside the windows.

When they reached the wall, they flattened themselves against it. Gregory took the kitchen doorknob in his hand and gradually turned it. For an agonizing minute, he stood, twisting the knob, lips sucked into his mouth.

"Locked," he said.

"Greenhouse," whispered Brian. He pointed around the corner.

They crawled around the corner on their hands and knees. When they reached the glass solarium, Gregory slowly rose, peering through the panes, through the fronds, into the dining room.

He nodded quickly. He turned the handle of the solarium door, and it opened.

The boys were inside. They stepped through the solarium into the dining room.

They could hear voices speaking in a strange tongue. Arguing. Someone was playing something hectic and terrified on the piano.

They moved toward the door to the kitchen.

Now, for just a minute, they could catch a glimpse into the entrance hall. Men in long, black coats lounged on the round, cushioned bench in the foyer. They were facing the parlor, watching whoever played the piano. Trailing all the way down the steps like a Christmas garland was what looked like a length of brown and gray muscle. Ripples went through it, and it caressed the wall.

Daffodil served drinks on a tray, her back to the boys, while off in the parlor, the piano trilled and thundered.

One of the men shouted with a strong accent, "She plays like a fawn! I should like to give her a locket, this pretty girl! Or tickets to a baboon show."

Prudence's voice, high and tight with fear, burst over the rumbling chords, "It is a piano sonata by Mr. Robert Schumann. It was first composed — "

"Mr. Grendle!" shouted the man. "I should like to see your stepdaughter dance."

The piano playing stopped. Gregory slipped into the kitchen.

Brian did not follow. He had heard that Prudence was sobbing. He couldn't move.

Uncle Max said something sharp in the foreign tongue. The man replied. Then Uncle Max and he were yelling.

Brian stepped quickly into the kitchen.

Gregory still waited there by the door.

Together, they stood hunched, listening to the argument in the other room.

"Daffodil," said the man with the accent to the maid, "move yourself about. Show us that fine profile."

Uncle Max protested.

"That's right, Daffodil. And you, too, Burk. Back and forth. Good. Good."

Uncle Max bellowed.

Then a gunshot rang out.

Brian and Gregory both gasped. Their eyes were wide. Their skin was white.

Brian moved to clutch the doorknob.

And the door to the kitchen slammed open.

They threw themselves in opposite directions — Gregory toward the basement door, Brian slamming sideways into a counter — and a figure stood between them —

Daffodil, holding her tray.

Half of her face was missing.

TWENTY-ONE

Don't," said Daffodil's corpse wearily, "go down in the basement."

Her cheek and part of her jaw were chipped off like porcelain. Below, they could see the spinning gears and heaving springs that animated her. Much of her arm had been blown off, too. She was a machine.

She saw them gaping at her. "Mr. Grendle's guests are using me for target practice."

Brian croaked, "Does it . . . does it hurt?"

"It is inconvenient," said Daffodil. "Without the arm, I cannot butter their bread." She stumbled to the marble countertop and dropped her tray there. The glasses slid and rattled. She reached up tentatively to where her cheek was missing. "I should put iodine on the cut. That is what my mother did."

"Daffodil —" said Gregory.

"Don't go down in the basement," she repeated.

"What?" said Gregory. "The Basement Lurker?"

She rolled her eyes stiffly. "Basement Lurker. Idiot child. That was a story your uncle told to keep your scaly hands out of his things. There is no such thing as a Basement Lurker."

"We need something from down there," said Gregory.

"No Basement Lurker, but it's crawling with spiky beasts," said Daffodil. "And the hunchbacked sentries are on the roof." She began clumsily transferring the glasses to the sink. "Everything has changed since you left," she said. A glass shattered.

The door slammed open. Prudence was in the kitchen, weeping dramatically. Her hands were over her face. The door swung shut behind her.

"Prudence!" hissed Gregory.

She looked up, startled. "Boys!" she said, and smeared the tears off her face with the backs of her hands. She held out her arms to embrace them. "I'm so glad you're safe!" she said. "I was so worried, after what happened the other night! What happened? What's going on?"

"We don't know," said Gregory. "There's an underground . . . it's really complicated. What happened after we left the other night?"

"Oh, it was very, very odd. There were noises everywhere, and I was sure that things were crawling all over the house — it was horrible! — and then suddenly Mr. Grendle just yelled something like, 'They're gone! They're gone! No rules have been broken!' — and suddenly, the wind died down, and all that rustling, and huge wings, and the croaking from the bathroom . . . they all just slowed down and just died away." She looked toward the door. "But these peculiar men came, and they're staying. We're putting them up in the guest rooms. They're always talking about a Game. When they're talking in English. They go upstairs to Mr. Grendle's office, and then they come back down and sit around and smoke."

"Who — who are they?" asked Brian.

"I don't know. . . . They're ever so peculiar," said Prudence. She touched her eye again. "They're horrible."

Gregory whispered, "We need to get into the basement."

"The basement? What for?"

"We need to get a bottle of your de-scentifying perfume."

She looked confused. "For out in the woods?" Then she smiled. "Have you met a little special someone?"

"Yeah," whispered Gregory. "He's about twenty-five feet tall, warty, and he stomps on his friends."

Prudence crossed her arms. "I wish just one thing you boys said made a grain of sense. I'll go get you a bottle from my room. Stay here."

She turned and took a deep breath. She took out a handkerchief and wiped at her eyes. Then she smiled brightly and stepped through the door.

Brian and Gregory stood awkwardly, watching the damaged Daffodil clean the dishes. Brian moved to her side to help.

She did not turn her head, but made a small sound like a warning bleat.

He stepped back, and she fell silent, scrubbing.

Gregory was listening at the door.

The man with the thick accent was saying, "Miss Prudence, we have placed our bets — but you, you have not placed your bet, yes? How is this, then: If my people win, you forfeit but the smallest kiss. Upon my cheek. Yes?"

"Excuse me, sir," she said. "I have to see about the maid. She seemed somewhat distraught."

"Miss Prudence," called the man. "Miss Prudence, a bet: If my people win, you spin in a circle quickly, and I may snap my fingers near your knees. Yes? Yes?"

She pushed the kitchen door open and then closed it behind her.

She had an atomizer bottle of perfume concealed near her side. She held it out to Gregory. "Here you are, boys. Good luck. I hope this helps. So you don't smell as brutish out there."

"Why don't you come with us?" said Gregory.

"I have to stay here with Mr. Grendle," she explained. "He needs me." She went to the back door and unlocked it.

"You can't stay here," said Gregory. "You're in danger."

She looked at him curiously. "I don't think I am," she said. "You are, though. They talk about you. I can hear them using your names. They're watching you." She pulled the back door open. A breeze came in from outside. "Maybe you shouldn't go back out," she said. "Maybe you should sneak away and leave."

"No," said Gregory. "We've got to go. We're going. Now."

Brian said, "Thank you for the perfume."

"You're welcome," she said. "Be careful." She kissed them each on the forehead. "Good-bye," she said. And then she added, wrinkling her nose, "You might want to try a little bit of that now."

They slipped out the back door.

Through the window, she watched them go, her white brow creased by a single line of determined concern.

✳ ✳ ✳

The two were melancholy and silent, staring morosely down at the branches they stepped over. Gregory wanted to say something cheerful about how they had overcome that hurdle with flying colors, but he didn't think Brian wanted to hear it.

After a long time walking, Gregory said, "Hey — think about what Prudence told us. When we ran out of the house the other night, when all those things were attacking — she says Uncle Max waited for us to leave, and then yelled out something about how we were gone, and how no rules had been broken."

Brian waited for an explanation.

"I bet Uncle Max summoned the Thusser," Gregory continued. "I bet he arranged for things to attack the house just when he was about to start really dishing."

"What do you mean?" asked Brian.

"Somehow, by asking Uncle Max what was going on, we were about to break the rules and forfeit the game. So he needed to get us out of the house before we could learn anything. So he called the Thusser somehow. By brain-phone. He summoned them. That's why he delayed us while we ate. He was stalling for time. He got them to chase us out before he could tell us anything important and break the rules."

They came to the bridge. They crossed over the river.

Brian crawled down the slope to knock on Kalgrash's door. Gregory waited on the bridge, scowling. The troll didn't answer.

Brian lingered by the door, his hand still in a fist.

"Come on," said Gregory. "We need to get moving."

Brian looked up at him skeptically.

"Let's go play the game. It's what he would want," said Gregory. "It's the reason he was built in the first place."

Brian didn't move.

"Come on," Gregory urged him.

Brian climbed back up and joined him back on the path.

They walked on without talking. The ground became hilly, and they passed into the Tangled Knolls. Brian directed them through the maze by pointing.

As they wandered through the Haunted Hunting Grounds, they heard once more the call of the horns, the answering cry, the baying of dogs. They looked around quickly, seeing only the wide expanse of tree trunks and lilies of the valley. Half-running, half-watching, they moved back to one of the wider tree trunks and put their backs against it. They looked one way, then the other, through the wood. The hunting horn reverberated again in the trees.

Suddenly, the hunting party broke forth again and

galloped through the forest. There, in the lead, were the clever-looking royalty of Norumbega — the young blond man smirking, the bishop in his miter, the others wearing circlets on their heads. They called to one another in some foreign tongue and rode past entirely ignoring the two friends, the rest of the cavalcade following behind in riding caps and wimples and top hats. Several small will-o'-the-wisps bobbed along behind, then faded out like the final sparks on a television screen.

Cautiously, Brian and Gregory stepped forward, glancing around them. Twigs snapped beneath their shoes. Nothing moved. The wind blew through the trees again, and leaves sifted to the ground. The two continued on their way toward Fundridge's Folly.

The folly looked much as it had when they had first found it. Dark leaves were strewn again across the floor, obscuring the peculiar mosaic and the capstone that covered the secret passage.

"Who moved them back?" wondered Brian, biting his lower lip.

"Speculant," suggested Gregory.

The dark-haired boy moved to shove the leaves off the capstone with the side of his shoe. Gregory stood with his hands in his pockets, watching his friend work. He said, "Hey, as a dog returns to its vomit, so doth a fool return to his folly."

The capstone was clear. Heaving, they lifted it out of its socket and dropped it once more on the tile floor with a crunch. Brian's pale face was red, and his collar had slipped. He pulled at the shirt and stuck his fingers behind the starched collar until it was straight. Gregory worked at lighting one of the lanterns. When they were ready, they went down.

The Speculant had listened to their complaint and brought the boat back to the Dark Marina. Once more, the two of them climbed in, unhooked the skiff from the clips on shore, and started up the ornate engine.

They drifted through the passageway that rang with the roar of their engine; they passed out onto the surface of Lake Gwarnmore. The noise of the engine was swallowed by the huge cavern around them.

The boat crawled across the surface of the subterranean lake. Nothing disturbed the surface of the dark water, although a thousand times, in the boys' minds, the boat was capsized by some heaving, coiled, glistening monstrosity.

Brian sat with the perfume bottle in his hands.

They heard a sharp crackling. There was light in the cavern. Green light.

They ducked low in the boat and peered over the side. It sloshed from side to side.

A fleet of ghost ships rode the waters, glowing. An orchestra played a weird symphony on a barge, a symphony shot through with dissonance, while dancers executed remarkable hops and leaps on a floating stage. Flags and pennants hung over the water, where synchronized swimmers in goldfish plumes spun their arms. On another barge, on a throne, sat the young blond man they had seen at the hunt, his crown glistening in long-faded sunlight. The music fluted through the cavern.

And then, with a snap, the vision was gone.

They were left in darkness. Brian was clutching the perfume bottle to his chest.

They sat back on their seats. The boat puttered onward.

After what seemed like ages, they passed beneath the ornate arch and went down the Taskwith Canal. Brian looked nervously at the prow, thinking of the beast that waited for them. Gregory made rhythmic tapping noises with his tongue and the roof of his mouth, sucking in his breath, impatiently drumming his fingers against the rim of the boat.

He turned around at the whiffling of the atomizer. Brian was smothering himself in the scentless perfume. His eyes were closed, and he squeezed the bulb again and again, spritzing it onto his skin and clothes. When he was done, and had squirted even his ankles, he handed the bottle to Gregory, and Gregory began to cover himself. They could smell nothing but wet stone. Gregory held up his arm and sniffed under it. Nothing.

Everything depended on that.

Finally, the boat pulled up to the Steps of Doom. Solemnly, the boys began to fasten the boat to the shore.

They got out. Snoring echoed from Snarth's Cavern.

They walked up the stairs. The ogre was curled up against the stalactites and stalagmites, grumbling to himself in his sleep. Gregory and Brian began to creep across the floor.

He shifted.

They froze.

His arm crept out from his body. The fingers were padding across the pitted floor.

Brian and Gregory moved softly toward the exit into the city.

The nose twitched.

The sleeping giant fumbled with his hand.

Rock grated beneath Gregory's feet.

Snarth snorted and lifted up his head. He growled. They ran. He rose.

He was standing, sniffing. They had reached the steps. He yowled. The echoes bounced around the room. Everywhere, there was the clatter of hard-heeled shoes against stone. The beast thrashed one way, and then another, feeling at the stone. He drew in great drags of air, his head thrown back. He charged one way and another across the cavern, smelling.

The boys had made it down the steps. They could hear the ogre thumping at the walls.

They ran down the street.

They could hear him headed the other direction, toward the boat — toward its tang of gasoline.

His footsteps faded.

Gregory held up his lantern.

They were alone, in the City of Gargoyles.

TWENTY-TWO

It was impossible to judge the size of the cavern that housed the City of Gargoyles. The dim beams of the lantern, when swung about, only served to reveal a few abnormally steep gables or a grotesque bit of statuary or an empty street — never any complete picture. There were no echoes. The dark void was vast and silent.

They began walking. Street after street of empty, stone-carved houses lay around them. Tiny alleys with lopsided, overhanging dwellings could be found next to wide avenues with large town houses. Everywhere, complex, steep roofs and towers flashed through the lantern light. On every window, on every lintel, on every chimney were wide grins and subtle sneers, growling jowls and slumbering lips, glaring eyes and blank stares — the expressions of a thousand intertwined gargoyles, elves, and beasts. The creatures wrestled with one another, they embraced one another, they crawled in vines and hung from swags of laurel. Some of the buildings, obviously shops, sported large carvings of their trade over their doorways: loaves of bread; fish strung through the gills on lines; woolens; scooters; furs.

Everything was empty inside. Whatever was there had rotted years before. A few of the buildings had collapsed long ago, leaving only a few twisted stone hands grasping out of the rubble as a clue to what once had been.

The first specter they encountered was in a town square. It appeared when they were admiring a statue in the center of the square — a stocky, strong-thewed man whose arms were crossed in disapproval.

"Looks like a Viking," said Gregory, noting the chain mail beneath the regal robes.

"Except for the ears," said Brian, wobbling the lantern at the figure's head. The ears were pointed and elongated, projecting from the great mass of braided hair and beard.

They stepped away from the statue, and there was a crackle of energy. Two people, a man and a woman, were sitting by them at a table, the man in a bowler hat. They took tea and glowed bright green. They spoke the runic language.

Gregory stumbled backward. The couple shut off like a light. Gone. The two friends looked around the square. It was dusty and empty, and looked like it had been so for centuries. They kept on walking.

Now the boys were on a great causeway where, in cobbled circles, trees had probably grown. Huge private palaces and houses were spread along the avenue, and white marble obelisks lined the sides of the streets. Carriages flashed briefly into vivid green life. Men and women were walking with parasols. Pointy-eared businessmen in high collars tapped the cobbles with their canes. When the boys moved on, the specters snapped off, and it was once again dark.

The boys found the dockyards, looking out over what was probably Lake Gwarnmore. Victorian streetlamps lined the pier. A stone dock with heavy iron mooring rings lay below, where once great ships had stood.

Abruptly, there were sailors there, glowing green, dressed in striped shirts, tossing crates to the shore, shouting orders to the rigging.

Later, high on a hill, they found a cathedral. Robed saints and angels, carved in white stone, posed in a thousand little alcoves, holding the symbols of their sainthood: here a palm leaf, a little ruined tower, a masquerade mask, a pair of blue jays, a pennywhistle. The great doors of the cathedral were slightly ajar, ringed by a choir of carved angels.

Beside the cathedral stood the castle, at the crown of the hill. A vast palace of steep roofs and gables, of slim turrets and parapets, rose across a chasm. A heavy drawbridge led from the cobbled square into the dark gate of the castle.

"Let's go," said Brian, walking toward the castle. Gregory followed him. They crossed the square, hard shoes clacking against the cobblestones, and started across the bridge.

Gregory paused on the threshold of the drawbridge. "This wood is new," he pointed out.

Brian looked down. Indeed, the slats beneath his feet

were of yellow, rather splintery wood, looking not older than a few months at most. "You're right," he said.

"Well, it won't bite us," said Gregory, shrugging, and they continued across.

Halfway to the gatehouse, unable to resist, they went to peer over the edge of the drawbridge. Although they shined their lantern down into the fissure, nothing but the uneven stone walls could be seen.

They continued through the archway of the gatehouse and into the courtyard of the palace. Dark gates and passageways led in all directions, winding away into the depths of the huge castle.

As they walked, the castle was filled with spirits. In the kitchens, chefs with windup keys in their backs labored over steaming cauldrons. In the vaults beneath, there were glowing barrels and bundles. Ghostly servants, wound up and ticking, walked among the crates, sifting through packing hay to pluck out jars of strawberry preserves or to draw forth bottles of Avalonian wine from moldy wine racks. As the two boys stared about, the vision faded.

In the ballroom, there was abruptly a ball. A dwarfish emperor sat on the throne, swamped by his robes and his crown and his ears, while around him, people curtsied and danced, and the band played, "Farewell, Fair Broceliande." The tiny emperor stood on his throne and pointed and shouted things, obviously tipsy.

In a bedroom, a counselor or statesman paced, frowning, dressed in a tight wig and long coat.

In another bedroom, there were two men who resembled Jack Stimple — dark rings around the eyes — the same grim look — Thusser — who wore sashes over their tailcoats. They had out a map of the city and were whispering together, as if scheming.

The rooms briefly sprang into phantasmal life as the boys passed through, and then, when they had gone, once more became dark and hollow. The ghosts seemed unaware of the boys' presence. Spirits wandered on the balconies over the dark city and giggled on the stairs. They practiced fencing in the courtyards. They fixed loose tiles on the slanting roofs.

The gardens were blooming again after centuries, with wide, translucent flowers. Fountains sprayed spectral water from their dry throats, and sundials glimmered in the light of a long-dead sun. Pointy-eared courtiers in long, silk frock coats strolled together and talked.

"These aren't ghosts," said Brian. "What we're seeing is the past."

"I can't take any more of this," said Gregory. "I'm hungry. I'm tired."

Brian nodded. "Let's eat," he said.

"Feasting hall, this way."

They went to the feasting hall and took out their sandwiches. There was a fireplace at one end, a minstrels' gallery at the other. The mayonnaise was getting ripe. On the wall hung an ancient tapestry of browning cloth. In the lantern light it was difficult to make out the details of the complex design, but it appeared to be a hunting scene. Determined-looking elfin creatures, dressed in Elizabethan costumes, rode through a cavern away from a white-spired castle; bats with little colored hoods hung from the hunters' heavy gloves. A rather small dragon-like creature slithered into a bone-strewn lair, glaring back at his mounted pursuers.

"What's next?" asked Gregory.

Brian shrugged.

Gregory said, "I wonder what Jack Stimple's up to."

"I hate to think," said Brian.

"Let's look at the board."

Gregory took the board out of his pack and laid it down. The City of Gargoyles was now drawn in fully, surrounding Lake Gwarnmore on two sides. A main avenue led up to St. Diancecht's Cathedral and, next to it, the Palace of Norumbega.

"Look," said Brian. "The finish line. We're close. Really close."

The finish square was right next to the cathedral. But in the space for the cathedral, it said, FINAL CHALLENGE. SOLVE RIDDLE OR LOSE TURN.

"Let's go," said Gregory. "Let's find out what this challenge is before Jack Stimple gets there."

"If he hasn't already," said Brian.

They went back down into the castle's courtyard and across the drawbridge. They walked across the square to St. Diancecht's, shining their light across the statues of saints and angels.

They pulled the great doors open. The vast nave of the cathedral was spaced out with pillars and sarcophagi. The two walked in, their footsteps whispering on the floor. Mosaic tiles formed spirals and sunbursts on the floor.

Ghosts flickered momentarily on phantom kneeling

pads, praying devoutly, then disintegrated. A few chanting monks, dressed in dark robes, drifted, glowing down the center aisle before fading away, their voices still echoing in the high vaulting of the cathedral.

Right before the altar of the cathedral was a marble statue of a king seated upon a throne. He had no face. The boys went up to inspect the statue. The crown, a slim coronet, was made of cheap, crumbling plaster.

"That's sort of strange," mused Brian.

"There's something written here," said Gregory.

"Hmm?" Brian moved in to look at the inscription as well.

I AM A KING WITHOUT A CROWN.

MY SUBJECTS ARE FLED AND MY KINGDOM THROWN DOWN.

FIND THE CROWN THAT LOOKS JUST THE SAME

AS THIS ONE ON ME — AND WIN OUR GAME.

At the base of the statue, near the carved folds of the king's robes, lay two metal boxes held together with duct tape, each with a red button on it. One was labeled GREGORY BUCHANAN, and the other one BRIAN THATZ.

"What is it?" asked Gregory.

"I d'know. They have our names on them, though."

Gregory picked the boxes up. "Should I push the button?"

"No," said Brian. "Put it down."

Gregory did, looking quizzically at his friend.

"Now," said Brian, "let's toss something heavy on it.

Something that will push the buttons while we're standing a little ways away."

They moved away from it. Gregory snapped at the buttons with his blanket. "My aim is usually perfect," he said. "I mean, with a towel."

He snapped the blanket again, and the button went down.

The boxes disappeared.

The boys stared at the empty floor.

"Great," said Gregory. "Great suggestion."

Brian went closer and looked at the space where the boxes had been. Nothing.

"Um," said Brian. "Sorry."

And then the boxes reappeared. Brian picked them up.

He and Gregory looked them over. "Hmm," said Gregory. "Looks like something you order out of the back of a comic book — s'posed to give you X-ray vision or something."

A row of monks faded into place before the plain stone altar, chanting quietly to themselves.

Gregory said, "Let's push the buttons."

"Both of them?"

"Where you go, I go," said Gregory.

They both put their thumbs on the buttons. They pressed. They waited.

The monks gained form and color. Torches and candles burned in iron candelabras all around the great cathedral, and priests wandered about in groups of two or three, whispering to one another.

"Excuse me," said the archbishop they had seen outside in the hunt. Now he was approaching them, dressed in his pointed miter. "Excuse me. No teleportation in the cathedral, please."

"Oh," said Gregory, choking. "Sorry."

"No problem. Just makes us antsy. And if you'd come in the middle of a service, well, that would have been more than a little bit embarrassing." The archbishop smiled lightly.

"Yes, of course," agreed Gregory.

"Oh, wait! You're the ones who are trying to save the world or something, aren't you?" the archbishop speculated, bobbing his finger at them while, with the other hand, he stroked his chin.

"No, no. We're playing a Game," offered Brian.

"Oh. Well, you told us you were trying to save the world."

"We'll say anything for a chuckle sometimes," said Gregory, mystified.

"Wait," said Brian. "When did we say that?"

"When you took the emperor's coronet," answered the archbishop. "A few years ago." He looked bewildered. "Don't you remember?"

Brian insisted, "Where were we? It's very important. Where did we get the coronet?"

"Oh," said the archbishop, "we were —"

The color drained from his face. He was pallid green. He had begun to glow once more. The candles faded, and the two boys were standing in the empty cathedral again, the ghost of the archbishop peering about, attempting to find them. "Hello? Hello?"

"Hello," called Gregory.

"Hello?"

"Hello!" insisted Gregory, running to place himself right in front of the archbishop. He waved his hands. "Hello!"

"Hello?"

"He can't hear you," said Brian. "We went into the past. Then we came back. He's looking for us hundreds of years ago."

Gregory turned, frustrated, reciting, "Five cents please. For an additional two minutes, insert five cents please." He crossed his arms.

The archbishop scratched his forehead and removed his miter to run a hand through his dark hair. He looked around, bewildered, then snapped his miter so it turned inside out. A new and more complex pattern was revealed. He put it back on his head, at a jauntier angle, and walked away.

"Hey!" said Gregory appreciatively. "His hat thingy is reversible!"

"Oh," said Brian. "What a neat idea."

The archbishop and his reversible miter faded away. The sanctuary was dark, save for the flickering light of the lantern that rested on the floor.

"So what are you saying happened?" said Gregory.

"We went into the past," said Brian. "Then we came back to the present. This little machine must send us back to whatever time we can see. We're supposed to go back and get the coronet."

"Whoa."

"Even better. We know that we are going to go into the past. Because by the time we were just in, we'd already gone back into the past. He told us so. So what we need to do is find the scene where we recognize the coronet, and go back and pick it up."

Gregory inspected the plaster coronet. "It has to be just like this one, huh?"

"Yeah," said Brian.

Gregory nodded. "Let's start looking," he said.

TWENTY-THREE

The trees were particularly bright that day. The air was particularly cold. As Kalgrash crossed the field, a blue-striped scarf wrapped around his neck and trailing behind him on the taller weeds, he sniffed and smelled the snow that would soon be falling. He kicked an acorn along the leaf-clogged path, watching it jump and roll unevenly.

He had sometimes considered setting off on a journey. From his youngest days, when he had looked on in indignation as, in storybooks, wandering knights had slain trolls, he had dreamed of wandering off, a few key possessions like his mug, his clock-under-a-glass-bell, and his silver tea ball slung in a pack on his back. He had dreamed of finding an evil knight and chopping off his head, just to even the score.

When he was older, he had sometimes had a more mature version of the same dream: the dream of putting everything away carefully in its place on the shelves and in the cabinets, of finally extinguishing the fire in his stove and cleaning out the ashes, and of taking that same pack, locking his front door, and rattling the handle to make sure it was locked, and of walking away. He would wander through the yellow wood, past houses that softly sighed smoke into the autumn sky, and he would leave the hills he knew; he would head into the world.

He had never quite figured where he would go. Perhaps he would go north, and cross the border to Canada secretly. He would continue north as little towns turned to single red cottages, then to just the occasional trailer spotted in the woods, then, finally, just the great wilderness, the bush. Perhaps he would make a pilgrimage to the North Pole, where his ancestors had lived. He would stand there in the snow, with the tundra ice-locked all around him, and feel the cold whipping by; and he would dance and sing where millennia ago the trolls had howled their songs at the northern lights. And then, perhaps, he would turn home.

He would trek back over the miles, back to those same woods he walked through now. He would walk across that bridge, and find his home dark, but as he had left it years before. He would only need to take the things off the shelves, to light the fires where the grates had been empty, and he would settle down with a book again and idly turn the pages, looking at the illustrations. He would spend the summers splashing in the water of the river, and he would tell his friends about his travels. And so things would go on. He had always thought of setting off on a great journey like that.

He passed through the Tangled Knolls. The forest floor of the Haunted Hunting Grounds glowed yellow with fallen leaves. They had not yet turned crisp here. They simply shuffled around his feet as he walked.

He continued onward, although the path stopped at Fundridge's Folly. He continued as the slope grew steeper, as boulders pushed their way with more regularity out of the ground. Finally, he pulled himself upward by grabbing tree trunks, the spiky claws of his feet clutching the rocks beneath him. The wind picked up as he headed up the slope.

He had decided that he would have to meet the man who had made him. He did not like to imagine what it would be like, what sort of feeling it would be to see the gnarled hands that had soldered together his heart and brain. He went, in a way, more to say good-bye than to say hello. He would meet the tinkerer, the Norumbegan who had designed even his teeth, and he would speak with him. He would prove to himself that he had surpassed his maker's expectation — that he was brighter, kinder, happier than any tinkerer could ever plan. Then he would coldly leave. He did not expect the interview to be a pleasant one. He would tell his maker how the Game had gone, what sort of things he himself had been doing since he was first wound and placed in motion, and then he would shake the man's hand and nod, and say good-bye, and walk down the mountain to return to his home, to return to his mulled cider and his fireside, but with a new start.

Thick groves of pine trees were sprouting up about him now. A little stream, padded with moss, ran beneath a wood of tightly woven firs. It was starting to freeze. Kalgrash could feel the clouds moving up from the south — he wasn't sure some magician wasn't pulling them up. He could feel them scattering snow over suburbs and cities, impatient to get to the mountains. He could feel the chill that they pushed before them.

At about five-thirty, he found the door in the boulder. There was the plaque that read WEE SNIGGLEPING and the tiny door into the enchanted workshop. There was a note tacked to the door that read GONE SKIING. The troll couldn't read it, but guessed its meaning.

A cold wind had sprung up. Kalgrash nodded slowly and grinned, although he didn't quite know why. He looped his scarf around his neck several times and looked out over the tops of the pines to the far blue mountains and the clouds that raced across them. He picked up a bit of granite with a sharp edge, then scratched into the door the symbol that meant his name — the only thing he knew how to write. He looked at the GONE SKIING sign and said to himself, "Okay." He tossed the rock up into the air, over his shoulder, and it landed in the pale grass. He began wandering down the mountain, against the bitter wind.

By the time he crossed the bridge over the River of Time and Shadow, it was blue evening and softly snowing.

✳ ✳ ✳

In the crypt below the cathedral, the boys found the tombs of emperors. Each had a likeness of the ruler sleep-

216

ing on its lid. Each was carved with the emperor's deeds. The first, whose statue they had seen in the town square, posed proudly on the prow of a leather ship as his fleet sailed over the clouds. Hovering above the sea, he hacked at a serpent with his ax. He hunted in the forests of primordial America. He built a scraggly set of towers on the mountaintop.

They passed an architect-emperor, holding a T square, compass, and plumb line. He frowned slightly, resting on his bier, as if he still worried about some matter left unfinished. The bas-reliefs on the sides of the sarcophagus showed him directing the construction of the City of Gargoyles.

Brian and Gregory walked down the line of emperors, watching as the Realm of Norumbega grew and battles were fought. They saw the coming of the Thusser — also men with pointed ears, but with lines scored under their sunken eyes. Gradually, the tunics and robes of those depicted in the carvings were replaced by knee breeches and long, buttoned coats. But always, the emperors in their resting place wore the robes of state first worn what must have been centuries before, when the first king came flying in his leather boat from the Old World.

They all wore the same robes; but each king wore a different crown.

The second to last was the little gray dwarf they had seen at the ball. He was lost in the robes of state. Their marble sleeves hung down the sides of the tomb.

The last emperor was the young blond man whom they had seen at the hunt. He was not slumbering on his tomb as the rest had been, but was instead depicted as if just wakened from a nightmare — sitting up, wide-eyed. He stared into a simple, dark, carved archway on the far wall.

The bas-reliefs on the side of his sarcophagus depicted him in various situations: in white tie, in the company of others similarly dressed, at a party; playing tennis in a V-necked sweater; sitting on a throne, a look of uneasy determination on his face, his finger jammed into his cheek to support his head; sitting in the forest with the other young men and women of the realm, wearing flat straw hats and drinking — and in the background, there were Thusser, watching. Then, abruptly, in the next panel he was dressed in a suit of armor, atop a crenellated tower, looking out over the forest. The mountains were coated in metal. A dark army gathered at the foothills and in the trees and in the sky, shaking weapons toward those on the tower.

The final frames were scratched into the stone by an amateur. They were little more than stick figures and boxy houses. They showed people stalking through the streets of the City of Gargoyles, wearing strange masks, holding guns that shot thick clouds of gas. The next showed the emperor deep in conversation with another crowned king, a king with sunken eyes, over what looked to be a chess-board. In the final one there was nothing but a picture of the city empty, with a trickle of water shown dripping through the cobbles.

The figure sat atop his coffin, the royal robes disheveled and slipping off his left shoulder. He stared into the darkness beyond the arch.

Crude letters were carved above the door in several languages. In English, they said STAY OUT.

"Come on," urged Gregory, heading toward the archway.

"Wait," cautioned Brian, but as his friend had already run into the next chamber, he followed.

Gregory stood in another room, down a short flight of stairs. On the far side was a black panel.

"Is that black place flat?" asked Brian. "Or is it a hole?"

Gregory shined his lantern toward it. No light shone within it. They halted, blinking. The void, abruptly, was laced with a blue spark. When it was gone, they were not sure it had been there. The darkness beyond the arch waited patiently.

Brian carefully made his way down the stairs and walked to Gregory's side. They advanced on the panel.

Gregory reached out to touch it. "It's a portal," he said.

Something moved near the ceiling.

Brian flashed the light up over their heads.

Something moved.

The beam tossed across it.

Descending silently were great messy globs of gray that hung on sprouting stalks like thick saliva hanging on a string.

Brian and Gregory stood, frozen, as the bulbs dropped slowly toward the ground and stopped their descent in midair at varying heights all around the boys.

Softly, his breath quavering with fear, Gregory started to move back toward the crypt, winding his way between the lumpy masses.

The sacks hung, silent; then, one by one, shuddered.

And as the boys watched, all around them, fingers and elbows pressed against the pulpy fabric of the sacks, and the cocoons began slowly to tear open. Brian yelped, and dodged through the hanging masses as blind, gray arms groped their way free and yanked hungrily at the air.

A hand pawed at Brian's coat. He wrenched himself away and jolted into Gregory. All around them the room was filled with uneasy motion, with popping chrysalids and fumbling arms.

"We'll never make it!" said Gregory.

"We've got to!"

"We'll —"

Brian had been grabbed — his legs tottered underneath him. There were chilly fingers on his face.

"Help!" screamed Brian. "Gregory!"

Gregory struggled backward. He grabbed on to the monstrous, lukewarm arm and yanked at it. Others were plucking at him now.

"Help!" Brian called again. He flung himself out of the grasp of one silent beast, but other arms were pulling at him, and Gregory was slashing all around him with his Swiss army knife.

It was a morass of wakening beasts, and they were in the center of it. The things were pulling themselves free. Now a leg was uncurling, starting to step tentatively on the floor. Jaws were biting at the Plasticine sacks.

"We're not going to make it!" said Gregory.

Brian yelled, "I'm summoning Jack! I'm using his emergency grenade!"

"No!" said Gregory. "We'll lose! We'll forfeit!"

"But if —" Brian started gagging. A hand was across his mouth. He fell to his knees.

He pulled the grenade out of the pocket of his backpack.

He felt teeth perched on his shoulder, ready to bite.

He threw the summoning grenade into the mob of crawling limbs.

It was time to lose the Game.

TWENTY-FOUR

There was a hiss and a blast of smoke, and through the tangle of alien bodies there was Jack Stimple, arms crossed, smiling. For a moment he did not even acknowledge the hands that nuzzled him dumbly.

Brian pulled the hand away from his face and jerked his shoulder out from under the teeth. He struggled forward.

"Jack! Help!" cried Brian. "Jack!"

"Brian Thatz!" he called. "Is that you?"

"Yes," said Brian. "Over here! Help!"

Jack Stimple reached into his pockets and drew forth some throwing stars.

He began to throw them at Brian.

The boy threw himself to the floor and watched the first throwing star cut into a nearby sack with a sickening smack. Gray blood drooled from the wound and splattered on the paving stones. Brian began to crawl across the floor, bending low as, above him, arms struggled free of the globs.

Gregory pulled himself across the floor just ahead of Brian. His lantern clanked along the floor. They saw Jack's feet pacing through the tide of chrysalids and arms and veiny legs.

A groping hand grabbed Brian's hair. He screamed in pain as Gregory crawled ahead. Jack turned and wove his way toward them. Brian caught a glimpse of Jack holding a knife.

Gripping his own hair by the roots, Brian tried to wrestle with the hand. His lantern fell to the floor and shattered. The hand jerked back; Brian threw himself forward, his eyes wild as the oil from the lantern exploded. The creature in the sack began to burn. The flames licked at the stringy webbing of the cocoons, catching, spreading.

The creatures jerked spasmodically as they attempted to rip free of their sacks.

Brian ran, half-standing, forcefully jostling his way through the tangle of cocoons.

Gregory had reached the top of the steps and was holding up his lantern, squinting into the smoke and crush of alien bodies, now freed and writhing. "Brian! Brian!" he shouted. "Brian?"

Brian forced his way out of the bags. Bodies — pale, strange creatures — were moving now about the room, completely free of the sacking that had held them.

Jack Stimple screamed. Gregory strained, but couldn't see what was happening to him. Brian was at the foot of the staircase, scuttling upward. Gregory reached down a hand and pulled Brian to his feet.

They turned to see the room. Great flames were billowing where the lantern had fallen. Indistinct nude figures moved about between the hanging cocoons, a few of which still shuddered with burning creatures trying to escape. A black tar of webbing ran slowly through the cracks in the floor. Jack Stimple was nowhere to be seen.

The two turned and ran breathlessly from the room, back into the crypt. Behind them, the fire blazed, the creatures mewled and screamed.

Now, a specter-show flashed on, glowing green — Norumbegans lined up, families, all of them sadly clutching a few possessions, dressed in long coats. An officer was checking them off as they passed into the room where the flames and screaming came from.

"They're going through the portal," said Gregory. "All of them. They're emigrating to another world."

"Let's get out of here," said Brian. They kept running for the exit.

Back through the cathedral they ran.

"Where are we going?" asked Gregory.

"Two choices," said Brian, puffing. "Two choices. I'm thinking . . . we saw that coronet two times on the blond guy — that last emperor — once on the Haunted Hunting Grounds, once on the barge out on the lake."

"Down to the lake!" shouted Gregory, and they forced their way back through the cathedral door. They clattered down the avenue toward the water.

The last emperor and the archbishop, glowing green,

sledded past them on greased platters. The emperor wore a knit cap instead of his crown.

"Boys!" yelled Jack Stimple from behind them. "Come back, boys! I was fighting the guardian creatures, not you! It's all a terrible misunderstanding!"

"Keep running," said Gregory. He looked at Brian. Brian didn't look well. He was breathing very heavily, his glasses slipping. They barreled past the weird facades of elfin palaces.

A metal disc whizzed past them and struck a pillar. The two charged breathlessly into the darkness, the lantern rattling in Gregory's hand. Brian stumbled forward as a metal disc buried itself in his backpack. They heard Jack Stimple curse behind them.

They turned into an alley and clattered along past grinning gargoyles, up tight staircases that led onto little courtyards; they could hear Jack pounding down toward them. They darted through a door.

Jack leaped into a house, following the glow of the lantern. Spirits sat around a great oval table, laughing and serving themselves beets and roast duck. Servants bowed and retreated, keys spinning in their backs. Jack looked around, then charged through a door on the far side of the room, through the illusion, disturbing it as if it were motes of dust in a sunbeam.

Out on the street, Gregory and Brian barreled through a grand parade. The band wore flat straw hats and striped blazers, and blasted some rousing, thumping tune ("The Mighty Flag of Murias"). Kids licked Popsicles and waved to brothers playing the tuba. Brian and Gregory leaped through phantom ticker tape, past a flower-strewn carriage that carried the gray dwarfen emperor. They hurtled through the Norumbega Girl Guides.

Jack burst out onto the street in the wake of the boys and stood, squinting angrily as the Norumbega majorettes smiled ecstatically and marched right through him. He plunged into the flute section, scampered through the pipe-organ-on-wheels, and raced along in the wake of the lantern as the parade faded, leaving only scattered bits of luminous confetti.

Brian and Gregory turned down a side street once again, vainly trying to keep track of directions. The lantern light bobbed along the dark walls, picking out mouths and fangs of stone.

Behind them, Jack yelled, "I'll find you! You need your light! I'll find you!" Then, a second later: "We're in the final turn of the Game, so I'm allowed to kill now! *I'm finally allowed to kill!*"

The boys stumbled out into a marketplace, and immediately merchants sprang up, carrying baskets and crates to and fro, shouting the names of their wares.

Brian pointed breathlessly to the statue of the Viking emperor. Gregory nodded vigorously, and they darted off to the right, toward Snarth's Cavern.

Jack Stimple looked about once again, confused by the glow of the tradespeople and their stalls, then set off after the boys. Lovers relaxed in sidewalk cafés; everywhere people were talking earnestly and laughing. Women were out with parasols. Acrobats rolled and jumped in the streets, tossing striped balls back and forth.

Brian felt another metal disc swipe past him. Jack Stimple was gaining.

Steel rang on stone as a disc skidded along the road, raising sparks.

Brian screamed.

Another shot through the air.

And Gregory saw it slice through the back of Brian's head.

TWENTY-FIVE

An instant later, five hundred years earlier, Brian and Gregory stumbled and tried to get their bearings. Brian had pushed the buttons and thrown them into the past just before the disk had hit.

Norumbegans dressed in Renaissance robes and Victorian morning coats surveyed the boys with distaste. Gregory and Brian pulled themselves up and raced down the street, the City of Gargoyles alive and at its prime all around them.

"Did Jack get through?" shouted Gregory.

Brian glanced back over his shoulder. "No. Just us."

"Then we're safe?"

"No! He can't touch us, but he may be able to see us! We probably look like ghosts to him — and we can't see him. When we switch back, he'll be waiting!"

Carriages clattered around the street. High above, the boys realized, a subterranean sun shone down on the dark stone of the houses. Pointy-eared Norumbegans with their mechanical servants filled the streets, tipping their top hats and skullcaps to acquaintances, stopping to peer at the wares of merchants. Gregory and Brian dodged through a maze of fruit stands, scrambling to avoid startled customers.

The end of the street was in sight — the wall of the vast cavern stretched upward, broken by the jagged entrance to Snarth's lair.

They ran up the steps. Snarth's Cavern, though dim, was lit with countless paper lanterns; it was a park, where wide bushes and trees grew out of cracks in the boulders. People strolled through the twilit garden along wide paths.

As Gregory and Brian reached the archway that looked out on the Taskwith Canal and the Steps of Doom, the paper lanterns began to fade. The shrubs melted. A stand of rhododendrons was unfavorably replaced by a sprinting Jack Stimple.

Snarth growled and reared to his feet, brute arms swinging.

Jack pointed one hand at him, and a blast of fire shot across the cavern. Snarth yelped.

The boys didn't stay to see the outcome. They could hear shouting behind them, roaring, thumping. They ran down the steps.

They leaped into the boat — it bobbed and bucked wildly, and water shot over the edge. Gregory yanked the clips out of their staples, placing his foot firmly on the shore, and shoved the boat into the stream.

Jack was running down the Steps of Doom.

Brian slammed down the starting lever, and the boat sputtered into action.

A metal disc stuck into the rim of the boat with a thud. Brian jumped and yelped. Jack was getting ready to throw another.

Brian held up the time teleporter. He pressed the buttons once again. It clicked.

Brian and Gregory dropped into the frigid waters of the canal, their boat gone. Gregory struggled out of his backpack, his eyes squeezed shut and his cheeks bulging with air. The water was so cold, he almost drew breath and sucked in water.

Brian struggled helplessly, flinging his arms out and gasping whenever his head broke through to the air. He could not tell what was air and what was water. He felt something shoot down his windpipe and gargle and choke in his lungs, and he screeched for breath.

A gondolier was lifting them from the water and carefully setting them down on the floor of the boat. Lanterns lit the wide canal, illuminating the way for various small vessels that were slim and high-prowed like the city's gables.

"Upstream," gasped Brian.

The gondolier did not understand English. Brian pointed frantically. Gregory added, "Please, very quickly. But not too quickly."

"?" said the man in his language.

"We want to stay near our boat."

"?"

"Our invisible boat! Oh. I guess never mind."

The gondolier looked mystified, but then shrugged, nodded, and began to row his gilded craft along toward Lake Gwarnmore.

"Sit up," Gregory ordered. Brian did so, looking considerably frazzled. His dark hair hung in thick strands over his eyes. Gregory crouched, and worked at pulling off Brian's pack. "Now you'll be able to swim better. Anything you need in there?"

"It's all wet," said Brian, puffing for breath.

The time-switch struck. They plunged back into the water. Gregory started yelling profanity. When they resurfaced, feeling the cold storm through their limbs again, they found that the canal was only lit by the warm glow of their lantern, which stood in the boat. They began swimming toward the boat, Gregory dragging the pack behind him. Gregory threw the pack over the gunwale and pulled himself kicking into the boat. He reached out and took his friend's hand, and with a heave, Brian tumbled in as well. They were both convulsing with shivers, their tweed clothes sopping, their collars sticky with wet starch, their ties plastered over their shoulders.

The boat puttered on toward Lake Gwarnmore, and the emperor's barges.

✳ ✳ ✳

They saw several visions as they crossed the lake: three-masted yachts, heavy with ornate nautical carving and webs of rope; square-rigged merchant ships, prowed with wood mermen; smaller skiffs; and even cruder, medieval-looking ships that seemed half-fortress. But the glowing rigging, the phantom mermaid figureheads soon faded silently, leaving the water dark and forbidding.

When they saw the barges with the dancers and the young emperor, Brian held the time teleporter at the ready.

"I really don't want to go into this water again," said Gregory.

"On the count of three," said Brian.

"Oh, sweet mercy," said Gregory.

"Ready?"

"They're all dancing."

"One."

"This is going to be embarrassing."

"Two."

"We're going to be really wet."

"Three."

They were in the water. The sky was lit with the subterranean sun. The orchestra played "Farewell, Fair Broceliande." Brian rammed into a synchronized swimmer. Gregory was heaving himself up onto the deck of the emperor's pleasure barge.

There was a whispering among the crowds on the barges. The orchestra played on. The dancers had stopped; Brian was standing among them. He looked awful, shivering, his soaked knickerbockers sluicing water that puddled around the dancers' silken tights.

The emperor called something to the orchestra conductor, and others repeated it. The music stopped. The courtiers were laughing.

The emperor asked Gregory a question. Gregory said, "I'm sorry to burst in like this? But we need your crown."

The emperor exchanged a look with a woman sitting at his side, who wore her hair wound in thick braids.

"The crown of the realm," the emperor of Norumbega said in English. "You would like to borrow it."

"That's right," said Gregory. "Your world is in danger. We're trying to save it."

Brian staggered forward, his teeth clacking. "We've come from the future," he said. "You must beware the Thusser Hordes."

"Hmm," said the woman. "Must we really?"

"Yes," said Gregory.

"Sirs," called the emperor to two Thussers who sat on gilded chairs, dressed in sashes. "Must we beware you?"

"Your Highness," said one, "you have nothing to fear. Continue with the dancing. There's nothing one likes so much as a rigadoon."

"Quite," said the emperor. "Hey — sirrah — soaked brat number one — explain: How exactly will borrowing my crown save the world?"

"We need to place it on a statue," said Gregory. "In the future."

"Yes. Of course." The emperor exchanged glances with the woman, and then with the archbishop, and then said, "Do I look like I have a hole in my head?"

Brian said, "It's absolutely necessary. You're going to flee into another world, and it's going to be up to us to keep your kingdom out of the control of the Thusser."

"I see. That doesn't sound likely."

"Please," said Brian. "We only have another few seconds here."

The woman leaned her elbows on her knees. "Oh, just give them the crown. I want to finish the dancing so we can get on to the s'mores."

"Swell," said the emperor. "S'mores."

"Your Highness," said the archbishop, "I cannot help but notice that — "

As he spoke, Gregory sloshed up to the Emperor of Norumbega, bowed, and yanked the coronet off his head.

"Pardon?" said the emperor.

"Sorry!" cried Gregory. "For your own good! Not much time!"

Windup guards ran toward him with pointed glaives. He grasped the coronet above his head with one hand and held his nose with the other. He drew in a big breath.

Brian braced himself for the switch back into the present.

The guards came to Gregory's side. They stood around him.

Everyone stared at one another.

Gregory let out his breath.

The archbishop cleared his throat.

"Ah," said the emperor. "Still here. This is a little awkward, isn't it?"

"Er," said Gregory, "say, whose cat is that?"

He pointed and fell through time, into the dark water.

TWENTY-SIX

The boys lay on the boat, exhausted and freezing. It was puttering toward the Dark Marina.

"We don't want to go back there," said Brian. "We have to get back to the cathedral."

"How?" said Gregory. "This stupid thing will just take us right back to the Steps of Doom, where Jack Stimple will be waiting for us."

Brian sat up. He reached over and shut the engine off.

The boat rocked in the stillness. "Not," he said, "if we just paddle to the shore."

"Our lanterns are wet."

"We can see by the light of the ghosts."

So they began the slow process of paddling with their hands and the game board.

Ships burnt into being around them and glowed for a few minutes, then faded away. The boys' hands were numb. They shivered as they rowed.

Eventually, they reached the docks. They clipped the boat to the moorings.

As they walked up through the streets, a later phase of history showed itself. Thusser warriors stalked past them, dressed in masks like crows' heads with glass windows for eyes; they held guns that looked like old-fashioned blunderbusses. Out of the wide nozzles poured bursts of gas.

On the hill up to the castle and cathedral, the last of the Norumbegans wandered with carts filled with antique chairs, with birdcages and babies and sacks of macaroni. They looked back over their beloved city. They were going into exile.

Then they flickered and were gone. The murmur of their voices remained for a while.

Brian and Gregory took a long time working their way up the avenue. They had to feel their way forward between ghosts. They swung their hands in front of them. Gregory carried Brian's wet pack. Brian carried the coronet and the time box in his pockets.

"I am sick," said Gregory in the darkness, "of wet tweed. I feel like I've spent the last week in wet tweed."

Brian wasn't feeling strong enough to talk.

They reached the square where the cathedral stood. Cautiously, they approached the building. They peered about within, watching green monks shuttle quietly through the apse.

"This is it," said Gregory. "On to victory."

They stepped inside.

Torches flared all around them.

Gregory said, "Here goes."

They walked toward the statue of the faceless king. Yellow light slid and shuddered across the marble.

"Almost there," said Gregory. He held up the coronet.

"Who lit the torches?" said Brian.

"I did," said Jack.

Gregory swore.

The two boys sprinted toward the front of the cathedral, where the statue stood. Jack appeared from behind a pillar. He ran to intercept them.

It was like a nightmare. There was no way to outrun him. He stood between the boys and the finish. Brian had the coronet clutched in his hand. His knuckles were white, his fingers red with the cold.

Jack came for him. Brian backed up. Jack lumbered onward — Brian screamed — Jack tackled him — and Brian threw the coronet away — toward Gregory —

With a thud, Brian hit the ground, his head slamming into the stone. Jack had his elbow in Brian's gut, his hands on Brian's throat.

Gregory scrambled to get the coronet from the floor.

"Now," whispered Jack to Brian, "death."

Gregory stood, the coronet in his hands, the statue to his left — and to his right, Jack Stimple killing his friend by shoving his thumbs into Brian's throat.

Gregory hesitated. "Hey!" he yelled. "Over here!" He started to run toward the statue.

Brian watched him. "He's going to win," he croaked triumphantly to Jack. "He's going to — win!"

"Yes," said Jack, pleased. "So he is."

"Gregory!" Brian gasped. The sneering face was inches

from his own. "He's almost there," wheezed Brian. "He's —"

"I know," said Jack Stimple. "Exactly."

Suddenly, Brian realized what was going on.

"No!" he screamed. "Gregory! Don't! Don't put it on there!"

Gregory wasn't listening. He was climbing the statue, pulling off the plaster crown and throwing it to the ground. In his other hand was the golden circlet.

"Don't!" screamed Brian.

"What?" said Gregory.

"Don —" said Brian — but he had pressed the button, and now both he and Jack Stimple had shot into the past and were ghosts to Gregory, their voices muffled, Stimple clutching Brian's neck, his hands moving to slam the boy's gagging head again and again against the stone floor.

TWENTY-SEVEN

Brian saw the torchlit world flung around him, felt the shock of his head banging the paving stones, felt the thumbs that slowly pressed into his throat, and he screamed. "Help!" he shouted. "Help!"

Monks came racing toward them, sandals slapping on the stone.

Jack lifted a hand and knocked a priest backward. He snarled and turned back to Brian.

"You're not our opponent, are you?" said Brian.

Jack didn't answer. He raised a fist.

Suddenly, strong hands were on his shoulders, hauling him off the boy, yanking him to his feet and holding him back.

"Take him away!" gasped Brian. "Quickly! Out of the building! Take him out!"

The monks looked around, bewildered.

"He needs to be as far away as possible when we

both . . . for when we both come back from . . . Take him away, please! Please!"

The monks dragged Jack Stimple toward the exit.

Brian stood. Others were watching him warily. Brocade cloths were on the altar. People were singing a mass. The statue of the faceless king was nowhere to be seen — it would not be carved for centuries.

Jack's shrieks were outside the sanctuary, now. Brian moved up toward where the statue of the king would be.

"Gregory," said Brian, "if you can hear me — *whatever you do, don't put the crown on the statue. We made a terrible mistake! Can you hear me? Gregory?*"

He waited. A monk padded up the length of the cathedral to question him. He watched the monk approach, and then suddenly fade. The cathedral was dark, cold, and empty. Feeble torches flared in the wall sconces.

"What do you mean?" demanded Gregory. He was poised to put the crown on the faceless king. "What do you mean?"

"Give it to me," said Brian. He ran to Gregory's side and pulled himself up on the base of the statue. "Give it to me now."

Jack Stimple's footsteps could be heard racing from the back of the cathedral.

"What's gotten into you?" said Gregory, holding the crown away from his friend. "What is it?"

"I'll explain later — just give it!"

"What's wrong?"

"Give it! Trust me! Not much time!"

Gregory looked in his friend's eyes. Brian was pale, and breathing almost in sobs.

Gregory said, "Brian. I trust you."

He held out the crown.

Brian took it and jammed the crown on the king's head. "Jack Stimple wasn't our opponent," he said. "You and I were playing against each other. You were the player for the Thusser Hordes."

They looked down, and saw that there was a block of stone at the foot of the statue. It said, FINISH.

It had not been there seconds before.

Brian flung himself down on the slab. He jumped up and down. He kicked the edge of it frantically. Clattering footsteps approached through the void of the cathedral.

A voice said, "It has been decided. Victory is with the People of the Mound of Norumbega."

But Jack Stimple still came on.

His footsteps slowed.

He stood before them. His eyes were downcast. His coat was torn. He had blood coming out of his mouth.

"So there it is," he whispered. "You've won." He looked at the slab beneath Brian's feet and repeated, "You've won." He walked right up to them. They shied away.

He dropped to his knees, and bent down to place his lips softly against the cool marble. He rested his forehead against the slab, his eyes closed.

He whispered, "I will not be forgiven for your victory, Mr. Thatz." He looked up, menacingly. "And now there is no one to protect you. No Game. No rules."

Brian started running.

"Mr. Thatz," called Jack. "You can't run. At least, very fast." He rose and cracked his knuckles.

There was movement in the shadows. Jack glanced that way. Gregory was running after Brian.

It was the Speculant.

"You can't stop me," said Jack. "The boy will die."

The Speculant slid forward. His limbs brushed and tickled the stone beneath his cloak.

Jack held out one arm toward Brian. He whispered words. The fingers twitched and glowed. Brian ducked.

The Speculant barked.

There was a blast in Jack's hand, and he was wringing out his fingers, swearing.

Brian and Gregory were moving more quickly toward the back of the cathedral.

The Speculant darted to Jack's side.

Jack kicked at him, spun, swung a fist in a roundhouse punch — but the Speculant dodged.

Lightning-quick fingers of bone wrapped around Jack's wrist, and twisted. Jack gritted his teeth, stumbling.

Another hand shot up to Jack's face. It clutched the features. It squeezed.

Jack could not move.

Other hands were coming out of the cloak now, plucking at a long piece of red cloth.

"No," said Jack. "Let's not do this. Let's not."

The Speculant was rattling his fingers up and down, winding cloth around Jack's eyes. "Don't," pleaded Jack. "Stop this."

Jack struggled. Hands held him. He twitched. The cloth was wrapped around his mouth, haphazardly in stripes across his chest, around his legs, around an arm. The Speculant kept winding him.

Jack Stimple could not be recognized. He had no face, but was blank, like a doll. Now he started fighting again, struggling against the cloth. He pulled it away from his mouth. His other hand was working at a pocket — withdrawing a little gilt box. He popped it open.

As fast as he could struggle, the Speculant wound him.

Inside the box was a pill. Jack threw it back into his throat and began coughing. "You won't deliver me to them," he said. His body jerked with his gagging.

The Speculant embraced him.

He fell.

The Speculant held him while he grabbed and quivered.

Finally, he was still.

The Speculant finished winding him.

He did not move again.

The Speculant looked up. "Go," he said. "You are done."

The torchlight bobbed on the walls.

"Game's over," said Brian. "Let's go."

Gregory nodded. They walked to the exit. They took torches from the wall. They glanced back to see that Jack lay still. The Speculant pulled at him. They passed out of the cathedral and crossed the square.

A voice repeated, "Victory is with the People of the Mound of Norumbega."

A light above clicked and flickered. The boys shielded their eyes as the great artificial sun burst into flame in the stone sky above them. Light poured all around the City of Gargoyles, highlighting every gable and shingle.

Ghosts were all about, oblivious to Gregory and Brian. Fanfares were playing from the balconies, and banners and tapestries were being unfurled. Trumpets blared over the city, and crowds cheered before the castle gates.

It was the memory of another victory.

The boys walked down into the city, toward the docks.

People were making merry on the streets. They jabbered in cafés, they hopped around chalk circles, they embraced one another. A parade was marching down main street, trombones and trumpets blaring. Children in school uniforms slipped through the streets, pinching and poking and pointing gleefully. People ate thick, doughy pretzels and roasted chestnuts. Several pointy-eared girls with ribbons in their hair bounced back and forth across swords in a complex dance, their hands on their hips.

"I guess we won," said Gregory, looking about him at the laughing, semitransparent crowds.

Brian grinned. "Officially, I won. You lost."

"Okay. Now explain this to me."

Brian said, "Jack Stimple — Balerond — was just here to act as an operative for the Thusser or something. He wasn't actually playing the Game. I suddenly realized that this was why he was more interested in holding me down than in stopping you. And that's why he kept on trying to convince me to quit, before he was allowed to kill us. And that's why he woke *you* up when he was climbing up to the roof — he wanted *you* to get the weathervane first. And earlier today, that's why he kept throwing the discs at me. He didn't want to hit you. You were on his side."

"Whoa," said Gregory. "You quick bunny."

Brian smiled. It felt like the first time in a long time.

Children licked lollipops, people threw cream pies, a boy blew a toy bugle from an open window.

Gregory and Brian reached the dock. The boat was rocking there on the shore. They unclipped it from its mooring and, once they were settled, turned on the motor.

"You know what?" said Gregory. "I'm glad all this happened to us. I mean, to you and me. An adventure."

"Yeah," said Brian.

"Friends for life," said Gregory.

Brian nodded. "Friends for life."

They were out on the lake, surrounded by ghostly galleons. Above the great city, fireworks exploded and bloomed, and the sun was shut off so everyone could see them.

Brian and Gregory, sitting in their puttering boat, clapped and said, "Ooh!" and "Aah!" appreciatively for the best ones that spread through the cavern's dome. The Norumbegans clapped and shouted in the streets, and gathered on their balconies and rooftops to watch the fireworks explode. In the darkness, girls turned to watch the light flash above the smooth faces of the boys who stood by their sides — and then put their hands over their ears to block the booms and shrieks of the fireworks.

The finale crackled and roared near the ceiling, spreading giant squid-arms over the crowds, sending dazzling tadpoles whizzing off into the sky. Everyone cheered, and the bands struck up "The Empress Danann March."

The boat passed on into the Roots of the Earth. Behind, the final booms ceased to echo, though the singing and laughing and drinking went on as the streets darkened and darkened even more, the happy specters slowly fading, their voices becoming indistinct and mute in the lanes and avenues, the past receding ever further into the past.

The City of Gargoyles was empty once again. Still streets stood beneath a black sky, the sun dead again. The courtyards were dry and cold. A body lay on the floor of the cathedral.

The boys clipped the boat to the shore at the Dark Marina and, taking the lantern from the prow, walked up the steps. Bitter cold blasted from the open trapdoor.

Outside, the snow had fallen thickly in the blue darkness. Great loaves of snow lay on the branches and boulders in the wood. The woods were silent, save for the patter of flakes as they dropped all around the folly.

A sleigh, and two horses to draw it, stood waiting with Uncle Max and Cousin Prudence warmly wrapped inside. "Come along," said Uncle Max to the boys. "Time to go home, have some dinner. Then I have a few explanations to make."

"That sounds like a very good idea, sir," said Gregory as he stepped into the sleigh.

TWENTY-EIGHT

The sleigh slid through the forest. Snow still fell softly.

Prudence asked them, "Are you all right? I was so worried about you . . ."

"We're fine," said Gregory quietly. "But Jack Stimple is dead."

"Dead? Who?" gasped the girl. "What do you mean?"

"Yes," grunted Uncle Max. "How did he die?"

"Committed suicide. He fought with the Speculant. The Speculant was wrapping him up in something. Then he took a pill. It was poison or something. Because he lost," Gregory said more softly. "Because *I* lost."

"Ha. Well. Can't get off that easily. His people will want him," the old man grumbled. He reached into his cape and pulled out the horn of an old-fashioned phone. He turned a crank and held the horn up to his ear, then his mouth. "Yes," he said into it. "Balerond's gone and offed himself. Yes. Make sure he's back in shape before you bring him to the house." He dropped the mouthpiece back into his pocket, shaking his head.

The sleigh wound its way through the woods — down the slopes of the Haunted Hunting Grounds, through the swerving pathways of the Tangled Knolls, across the dark wood, and finally through the Golden Field to the River of Time and Shadow. Flakes fell on the black water and were swept soundlessly away on the ripples. The sleigh scraped across the bridge, the horses' hooves clomping loudly on the boards that lay beneath the lightly packed snow.

They bumped on, past Clock Corner, through the depths of the wood.

The house was lit across the lawn — great trails of light led from the windows across the snow. The sleigh pulled to the front of the house, where Yockly the carriage driver waited, huddled in blankets on the veranda. He silently hurried forward to take the reins. Uncle Max stood and slapped his gloves together vigorously, then stepped out and started for the house. The others followed nervously.

Burk and the damaged Daffodil waited inside to take the coats. Uncle Max swung his great cape off his shoulders and draped it over the butler's arm, following with his top hat. He said to the boys, "Go up and change. Dry off. We'll wait for you."

When Brian and Gregory came downstairs again and went into the dining room, they found several of the strange men sitting around the table with Mr. Grendle. All were dressed in white tie, and all had elfin ears. Most of them looked like Thussers.

Uncle Max indicated the boys. "My nephew, Gregory Buchanan. His friend, Brian Thatch."

"Thatz."

"Not really worth correcting now," said Uncle Max.

One man, a bony gentleman with sunken eyes, rose and held out his wrinkled hand. "So nice to meet you at last," he said, an ill smile on his face. "Count Azelwraithe."

"Nice to meet you," said Gregory.

"Our player," said Count Azelwraithe. "I've heard so much about you and your . . . little escapades."

"Oh. Really?"

"Yes, everyone's talking about them," he said sourly. "Please, take a seat." He indicated two free places.

The boys sat, looking from one oblivious face to the next, completely confused. Prudence sat, looking shyly at her plate.

The dinner seemed to take forever. The men jabbered at one another in their runic language. No one spoke to Prudence or the boys. The servants were half-broken, the gears whirring beneath their cracked and splintered faces. When the beets were being served, Burk coldly announced that Mr. Balerond was at the door.

The Thusser entered weakly, his limbs stiff and his dark coat littered with snow. When he breathed, there was a slight whine like that from a leaky balloon. He coughed and, in a bitter, dim voice, apologized. "I'm . . . so sorry to be late. You know I wouldn't want to miss . . . even a minute of such . . . a distinguished gathering."

"Ah, Mr. Balerond," said Count Azelwraithe. "So nice you could make it. Come sit by me. We have so much catching up to do. I have no idea what you've been up to since we last spoke. Really. No idea at all."

Jack Stimple shuffled across the floor to the seat offered him, pulled the chair out with several loud bumps, and managed to sit stiffly. He glowered at the boys across the table, then averted his eyes. His breathing whined, as if through a hole.

Everyone ate.

After dinner, the guests left. They thanked Uncle Max in their jabbering language, pulled on capes and greatcoats, and set off into the night. At the door, Count Azelwraithe bade the boys farewell as he left. "Yes, well, really. Thank you for an excellent round. So well done. It's a pity we couldn't stay and Play longer. Well, 'Mr. Stimple' and I simply must go. The Game, my dear Balerond, may be over, but the fun hasn't yet begun." He glared at Jack Stimple. "Thank you all for a most entertaining time. Good-bye, now." He bowed and stepped outside.

"Good-bye," muttered Stimple, and he turned slowly and tromped after his master.

"What will happen to him?" asked Gregory as Daffodil shut the front door and turned the lock.

"Never mind that, boy. You're like a damned journalist. Ridiculous sensationalism." Uncle Max turned and walked into the parlor, then sank into his favorite chair by the fire. Prudence, Brian, and Gregory stood nervously in the front hall.

"Come in!" shouted Max.

They went in.

"The Game is over. Sit down." The three arranged

themselves on the couch. Uncle Max lit a cigar, working his cheeks to puff smoke, and settled back in his chair. The grandfather clock slowly ticked.

Uncle Max rose from his seat and faced the fire. He picked up the poker and prodded the logs for a bit. He drew in a breath and began. "There has always been a race that has hidden itself from the eyes of men." With a rattle, he dropped the poker back into the stand. When he had seated himself, he continued. "Where they came from . . . don't know. Seems unlikely they evolved as we did — suspect they came from another world. They lived alongside men for thousands of years, their ways and homes hidden from ours, but always just around the corner. Men called them by all kinds of names. Sometimes men mistook them for elves. Foolish mistake to make. Still. They split into various empires, spread across the world.

"Came a time, though, when men refused to have anything to do with them. Things became difficult. One group of these Fair People set off for the New World. Maybe two thousand years ago, maybe one thousand. I don't know. A prince of this race, Durnwyth Gwarnmore, sailed through the sky with some settlers, came and built a home on the mountaintop here. Started a new empire. Called Norumbega. The Realm of Norumbega. Before a few hundred years passed, he'd been followed to the New World by others. Most notably, the Thusser.

"The People of the Mound of Norumbega, they were always fighting with the Thusser. Various territories were lost and gained, so forth and so on. Years went by.

Make a long story short, the last emperor came along. Young man. The beginning of his reign seemed perfect. A golden age. The Thusser were lying low, see. The People of Norumbega had been getting more and more carefree. Paying less and less attention. The last emperor did nothing to recall his people to the crisis that was brewing."

Uncle Max rested his heavily lined forehead in his hand and, gazing into space, explained, "One day, the Thusser were on the march. The emperor armored the mountain itself . . . typical excess . . . metal all over the mountain, all the guard towers manned, big blunderbusses and cannons mounted on dragon-back. Ridiculous. The Thusser surrounded the mountains. Superior firepower. No interest in picnics. There was a stand-off that lasted a year or so. Very few shots fired. A siege where nothing happened. It looked like sure defeat for Norumbega. But it looked to both sides as if it would be a long and costly battle. A battle that could take years. Difficult.

"So the last emperor of Norumbega sent a message to the king of the Thusser, saying that it would be crass to actually engage in battle. It would be very human. Which is not a compliment to these people. He proposed a Game. A sort of conditional surrender.

"The Thusser agreed, under certain terms. Essentially, they won. The Norumbegans, their empire fell apart. They were forced to leave their homes, to flee exiled through a portal into another world. Yes, you came close to destroying yourself by following them. If you'd gone through that panel into Beyond . . . the Guardians stopped you in time, however. Dropping from the ceiling. Yes?

"So the People of the Mound of Norumbega disappeared from this world, leaving their city empty, as agreed by the treaty. And it was decided that a series of matches would be played. Best of twenty. If the Norumbegans won most matches they'd get their kingdom back. Otherwise, each time they lost or forfeited, the Thusser would claim part of their territory. The Game would determine it all. The players, or the pawns, would be humans. They couldn't be told about the Game. There had to be ways of provoking them to Play. That explains a lot of what you've seen. Things to startle you, to get you moving. Like the dream you both had of the mountains covered in metal — quite simple, just a special kind of film. Nothing more embarrassing than Players who won't Play. If you had left, the Thusser would have taken it as a victory — which is why I tried to keep you playing, and Jack Stimple tried to keep you running.

"The Game is not only played by humans, it's arranged by a human, working within the rules set out by the Thusser and the Norumbegans. Each winner sets up the Game for the next players. This time, it was decided we should come back here, back to Norumbega itself, for the five hundredth anniversary of the treaty. We repopulated the mountain. We used the flimsiness of the world wall here to create the time fluxes and so on.

"Of course, there were some casualties. Not just people who stumbled onto something from another world. But one man who actually stumbled onto one of the rituals used to activate the time-slips and the board itself. He went mad. Starved to death. Eaten by beasties.

Don't worry about him. He won't be missed. Real estate developer.

"So you played. You won. Good. The Thusser have been brought to a halt for this round. The Game continues. You'll have to continue it, Mr. Thatch — the next round will be yours to invent, when you choose. Future years, that kind of thing. Give it a rest for a while. You're the nineteenth game of twenty. The chain of players has gone around the world, gone through the centuries. The Game has taken all sorts of forms. I've only heard about a few. An island of marble that floated on the sea. A kingdom of goblins that lived in empty New York warehouses and sewers — fellow thought he had to rescue some society damsel from them. She rescued him, married him, too. Let's see . . . Museum whose doors were suddenly locked one day, whose exhibits kept getting stranger and stranger . . . a shining castle that rose from an Iowa corn-field. They go on. Generation after generation." He said softly, "Player after Player, pawn after pawn. . . ." He scowled, and tapped his forefinger thoughtfully against his knee.

"So you won the Game last time, and had to set this one up for us?" Gregory asked.

Uncle Max looked up. He stood and tossed his cigar into the fire. He leaned wearily against the wingback chair. He reached up to massage his scalp. The hair flexed beneath his fingers.

He lifted up the top of his head. Wheels and gears spun there, glinting in the light.

"No," said Prudence. "I did."

TWENTY-NINE

W hat?!?" gasped Gregory.

"I stumbled onto the Game when I was traveling around the world, after my parents died. I was in Crete, walking along the beach, when a centaur approached me and showed me the way to the Labyrinth. I won there. I decided to come back and see the ruins where the Norumbegans had originally lived, and I found the Ceremonial Mound out there, and the rock with the carving all over it. Finally, the remaining Norumbegans agreed to show me the City of Gargoyles. So I decided to do the five-hundredth anniversary match here, like Mr. Grendle just explained. I moved into a house nearby — the house you found — and I started to make creatures and obstacles with them. Like Mr. Grendle — we made him first. I had always liked Victorian novels, Gothic novels especially. So that was what my Game was like. I got the Norumbegan craftsmen to make the things I needed, the servants and so on. You'll have to do it, too,

Brian. It's one of the privileges of winning. The winner of your Game will determine who gets these mountains. Then the Game will end, I guess. The spirits can wait."

Gregory said, "So you knew about it all along?"

"Yes, of course. Mr. Grendle and the Speculant took care of watching how things were going, and I just relaxed — oh, please, Gregory, did you really think I was as sweet and boring as I pretended to be?" She laughed.

"Well . . . I guess . . . um, when I'd seen you before, years ago, I'd sort of gotten that impression. . . ."

Prudence laughed once again. "What did you expect me to do, my dear? We only met at Thanksgivings and Christmases — uncomfortable times of the year for someone whose parents have died. If you were faced with some eight-year-old who kept making dumb jokes and hitting you with his Tinkertoys, I don't think you'd exactly be dazzling and charming. . . ."

"But —" Brian protested, "But how about the way the Thusser were threatening you when we came back to the house to get the perfume?"

"They're not nice, if that's what you're asking. But mainly, that was all a show for your benefit. We were anxious it was taking you so long. You were running out of time. The two of you refused to separate. You wouldn't play against each other. We wanted to speed things up, and we decided that if you thought I was in danger, you'd take the whole thing more seriously."

Gregory was shocked. "You knew we were coming? How did you know?"

Prudence reached out and cupped her hand over his knee. "Honey, honey, you walked across an acre of lawn in broad daylight."

"You weren't really crying?" said Gregory.

She smiled. "Sweetie, you were already so frightened and confused, I could have said, 'Boo hoo, boo hoo,' and you would have believed me."

"So we were supposed to be competing against each other the whole time?" asked Brian.

"Your friendship," said Prudence, "was a real obstacle. But now the whole thing's over."

Uncle Max turned from the fire and stolidly sat. With a soft screech of metal on metal, he screwed the top of his head back on.

"Well, dears," said Prudence, "you've won. Congratulations! Now it's time that we cleared out. Why don't you go up and see if there's anything you want out of your room. I shipped my things off earlier. I'm going to change out of this dress."

The two nodded and stood. They went upstairs to the nursery as if in a daze. The beds were stripped bare. The toys were gone. Brian looked out the window at the woods. There was nothing unusual there.

Below, in the front hall, Prudence, now dressed in jeans, a T-shirt, and a heavy sweater, sorted through the things in the boys' backpacks until she found the Game board. She rose and took it into the parlor. She stood before the fire, Uncle Max staring blankly past her, and cradled the board in her slim arms. She brought it briefly up to her lips. "Good-bye," she whispered. "It has been fun." Her arms went slack. She opened the board up, glancing across the bright colors of the completed paths . . . the Dark Wood, the Troll Bridge, the Club of Snarth, the Ceremonial Mound, the City of Gargoyles itself. She closed the board slowly and let it slide from her cool fingers into the flames. For a moment, it squelched them, but then they recovered. They licked the edges and, finally, they grabbed hold of one corner of the board and blackened it, and began the slow crawl across the surface.

The boys were at the foot of the steps, their hands dangling at their sides. "Wrap up warmly," she said softly. "It's snowing very hard, and it will be a long way to the station."

She darted back and kissed her uncle Max on the forehead before she left. "Good-bye, Mr. Grendle. Thank you for all of your help."

He patted her lightly on the shoulder and nodded. He could not speak. She left him sitting by the fire.

She opened the door. Outside, the snow was falling thickly but slowly, drifting down to settle on every edge, to cover every branch. "Out now, you two." The boys stepped out onto the veranda. Prudence called back in, "Burk, will you extinguish the lights and lock everything up? Thanks, you're a sweetie. Good-bye."

She pulled on her coat and put on her gloves. "Come on," she said. She closed the doors, and they walked down the steps.

The troll was leaning against one of the pillars by the front porch.

"Kalgrash!" exclaimed Brian.

"Hiya. The Speculant mentioned that you'd won the Game. Hey, congratulations." He blew a bugle noise through his fist. "And sorry to hear about you, Gregory."

Gregory dipped his head. "No sweat." He extended his hand. "Well, it was nice knowing you."

"Yeah. Nice knowing you, too." He shook the boy's hand.

Brian said, "We're sorry. Again. About."

The troll shrugged. "Oh. No. Well. Had to happen sometime. Now I know. That's it."

There was a silence. Finally, Gregory asked, "So . . . so what will you do now?"

"Oh, lots of things. There are leaves to rake . . . croquet to play, and tea cozies to knit . . . and there are dams to build downriver, and trees to plant near the highways. There are always a lot of chores to do in the wintertime. Maybe someday I'll go on a trip. I'm thinking about it." He smiled. "I'll get along. I know the worst now. I know I'm not alive. So now I can start to live."

"Well . . . we'll write sometime," said Brian.

"Okay. That'd be nice. I'd make up what the words mean." The troll grinned. "See, it's much better if you don't know how to read. Then you can make the letter say a different thing every day. It's like a whole lot of letters." They stood in silence, the snow falling all around them.

"Well, bye then," said Brian, shaking the troll's claw.

"G'bye."

"Good-bye," said Gregory again.

"G'bye."

The troll waved, turned, and walked behind the house,

his great feet crunching through the thick snow. His dark green skin faded into the night itself as he wandered back out through the woods to his warm home beneath the bridge.

Prudence, Brian, and Gregory continued to walk out toward the road. The sleigh was waiting for them. They got in and sat side by side. Prudence pulled a blanket over their legs.

The house was dark behind them, snow piling on the peaked roofs and shingled turrets. Brian looked back toward it. Prudence said quietly, "The house will fade soon. It's not real. None of it's real." The horses pulled, and the sleigh started off toward the road.

"I feel horrible about Kalgrash," whispered Brian.

"Yeah," agreed Gregory.

"Now, now," Prudence said softly. "Don't worry yourselves about it. It's just a silly game. Just a silly game." Prudence stroked Gregory's cheek and bent to kiss him gently on his head.

The house was falling to pieces silently behind them, as if the walls were soaked toilet paper, ripping and sagging beneath their own drenched weight. The snow tumbled in to bury the remains.

They turned for the last time from the house. Prudence put her arms around the boys' shoulders and shook the reins, and the three of them started along the road back into town.

After a time, she started singing, and for a long while, her carols drifted back through the leagues and leagues of dark forest, and of softly falling snow.